UNDERGROUND

UNDERGROUND

TONY DOBINSON

Scripture Union

By the same author:
He should have looked behind him
Hooked
Ready-made assemblies about famous people

Copyright © Tony Dobinson 2002
First published 2002

Scripture Union, 207–209 Queensway, Bletchley,
Milton Keynes, MK2 2EB, England.
Email: info@scriptureunion.org.uk
Web: www.scriptureunion.org.uk

ISBN 1 85999 601 9

Scriptures quoted from the *Good News Bible* published by The Bible
Societies/HarperCollinsPublishers Ltd., UK, © American Bible
Society, 1966, 1971, 1976, 1992.

British Library Cataloguing-in-Publication Data.
A catalogue record of this book is available from the British Library.

Printed and bound in Great Britain by Cox & Wyman Ltd, Reading,
Berkshire.

*Scripture Union is an international Christian charity working with
churches in more than 130 countries, providing resources to bring the
good news about Jesus Christ to children, young people and families
and to encourage them to develop spiritually through the Bible and
prayer.
As well as our network of volunteers, staff and associates who run
holidays, church-based events and school Christian groups, we
produce a wide range of publications and support those who use our
resources through training programmes.*

1

They appeared as soon as Joe and his father began to pull the kayak up onto the beach, a string of men on the cliffs, gazing down in silence. Joe knew they were armed, they always were.

Who had they come for? He looked left, then right. There was no one else around.

Then he understood.

He jammed his eyes shut, tried to stop himself shaking. But all his muscles seemed to be doing some crazy dance inside his skin and they wouldn't stop.

'Steady, Joe,' his father said, putting his arm round his shoulders.

Joe didn't want to look into his face, didn't want to see confirmation of his fears. So he looked up at the cliffs again. They were still there. But now one of the figures was moving, a man in a grey raincoat, making his way down the wooden steps to the beach. The unbuttoned raincoat was ballooning up behind him, making him look like a bird of prey, a vulture maybe, moving slowly in for the kill.

Now he was coming across the stones.

'Dad, the kayak – we could still—'

'No, we couldn't, Joe.' He sighed, a sigh that seemed to Joe could have blown away the cliffs, the soldiers, the sky itself. Finally, he looked at his father, but he hardly recognised him. His face seemed thinner than ever, more hollow, and he had almost shut his eyes like he was gazing at the sun. 'Joe, I'm sorry,' he murmured.

But Joe didn't want to hear, 'sorry', he wanted to hear, 'Let's go, let's make a run for it.'

Too late. The man in the raincoat had reached them now. He had a long face, the flesh on it sagging, as if his claw-like nose and spike-sharp eyes had punctured it from the inside. Yeah, though Joe, a vulture all right.

'Andrew Collins, I am arresting you as a corruptor of society under Law 240 stroke 5. Please come with me.' Then he looked at Joe, seemed to take in his presence for the first time. 'We didn't realise your son—'

'You'll take him home then. He's nothing to do with this.'

The man paused, his face expressionless. 'No,' he said finally. 'Both of you, follow me.' Then he turned and began plodding back over the stones.

'What do you mean, 'no'? He's going home or I—'

The man stopped, turned to face them. 'Mr Collins. I don't know if you realise the gravity of your position. You cannot make conditions. Now, please, follow me.'

'I shall not move until I have your promise that my son—'

'Mr Collins. Don't you understand?' Now there was a sharpness in his voice and his eyes were glinting. He lifted his arm, the raincoat flapping below it. Up on the cliff, one of the soldiers responded to the signal by raising a rifle to his shoulder. 'I have the law on my side, and the means to enforce it. What do *you* have,

Mr Collins?' He lowered his arm, pulling the coat around him. 'Now, as I said, follow me.'

They felt the telescopic sight of the rifle trained on them as they followed the man up the beach. Joe was finding it hard to breathe, his throat seemed blocked like someone was pushing his fist down it. It was pain like he had never known before, the worst kind of pain, the pain that comes from intense fear.

His father's hand was still on his shoulder. Behind them, the waves continued to wash round the forgotten kayak.

2

Two hours earlier everything had been normal. Joe's dad had driven down the bumpy path to the stretch of green at the cliff's edge, just as he always did. Then, with only a single squawking gull for company, they'd unstrapped the kayak and carried it down to the sea.

But nothing was normal now.

They reached the top of the steps. The soldiers were standing nearby in a group. The rifle had been lowered but was still held ready for use. There was no one else around: no one to see this happen. The vulture-like man with the raincoat pointed to a van parked on the other side of the green. It had 'Davis and Mills: Painters and Decorators' painted on it.

Joe could see their own car parked a little further over, pointing down the path that led to the road. Dad! his thoughts screamed. The car! We're parked facing the way out – they're not! We could do it! Dad!

'Perhaps I should have your car keys now,' said the man, as if reading Joe's mind. Taking his hand off Joe's shoulder, his dad got the keys out of his pocket, clutched them for a moment, then threw them to the man.

'Thank you. Now get in the van, please.' He signalled to one of the soldiers who came across and collected the keys.

But his father didn't move. 'It would be best to take the boy home now. The more he knows, the more problems you could have later. You must surely see—'

'I see the van, Mr Collins, and I see that you are not in it. I have a schedule to keep to, we will discuss all this later. Now, if you please.'

Joe had been admiring his father's resistance, but now he felt the hand on his shoulder steering him towards the van. Why had he given up so easily? Well, if his dad wouldn't… He shrugged off the hand and looked around: they were near the trees now – he could run, raise the alarm, find people who'd do something…

But even before he heard his father whisper, 'No, Joe, don't', he knew it was impossible. For the shakes hadn't quite gone and he still couldn't breathe properly. It was hopeless.

They came to the back of the van. There were no cans of paint inside, no brushes, Joe didn't think there would be. Just two benches facing each other. He had one foot on the step when there was a sharp noise above him. A seagull had swept low and now wheeled above their heads screeching. Joe wondered if it was the same one as when they arrived. Then it flew off over the trees and was gone.

He sat behind the passenger seat. His father sat beside him and went to put his arm round him, but Joe pulled away without looking at him. He didn't want to be hugged, he didn't want to be comforted – he wanted his father to kick up hell, not just give in to the Vulture's schedule. He hated it that his father had been interrupted like that. He was fourteen, just fourteen, but he wouldn't let anyone speak to *him* that way. And he hated that plaintive tone in his dad's voice when he'd said, 'No, Joe, don't.' Why was Dad letting himself be pushed around? If only he could stop the shaking, he'd show them...

One of the soldiers had opened the driver's door and was putting on overalls that were on the seat. Then he got in. The Vulture got in the other side, the back of his head by Joe's face. Joe could smell the hair gel. It made him feel sick. Then three soldiers got in the back and sat opposite them. As the door was pulled shut, Joe glimpsed two more going down the steps to the beach. The van began moving. It turned, started down the path through the trees.

'Dad, what'll they do to the kayak?'

But his father wasn't listening. He had his eyes shut and his lips were moving. Well, look at that, thought Joe. Praying, he's praying! As if that would help. But, yeah, that was his dad's response to anything bad – pray. Joe hated the idea. It was a cop out. He loved and admired his dad and wanted to tell him, 'You don't need those old superstitions – it's 2026, not the Middle Ages. Face reality, Dad.' Now here he was again, shutting out the real world, mumbling into the air, asking some higher power to take on his responsibility. Just a cop out.

He glanced across at the soldiers. One of them was looking at his dad and grinning.

The van had reached the other end of the path now. A soldier was standing there, next to a sign nailed to a tree. At a signal from the Vulture, he wrenched the sign off the tree and came across. Joe could read the words: 'No Entry. Military Training in Progress.'

'Anyone?' said the Vulture.

'Woman with a dog. No trouble.'

'Good. They'll be along soon with the car.'

Our car, thought Joe, as the van pulled into the road. The car you've stolen… He was feeling angrier by the moment. He glanced up at his father again. Still praying. It was up to him then.

He took a deep breath. 'Where are you taking us?' he shouted, aware that his voice sounded high-pitched and ragged.

Only one person even looked at him. The young soldier by the back door. At first Joe couldn't recognise the expression on his face: it wasn't hostility, or indifference. It was – yes, guilt, as if he'd done something he was horribly ashamed of and always would be. Then the face went blank.

But that moment, that look, confirmed the thought Joe had been desperately trying to push out of his mind since he saw the soldiers on the cliff. He couldn't do it any more: now he knew, knew for sure what was happening to him and his dad. They weren't being taken somewhere for questioning. Nothing like that. No.

They were becoming the Lost.

The rumours about the Lost, as they were called, had been going around as long as Joe could remember, but he'd never taken them seriously. Just the year before, one of the last times his father had got him to go to church, the pastor had said how his brother, who headed up some charity to help the homeless, had just disappeared on a walking holiday in the Lake District. He'd gone off on his own one day and never come back. According to the pastor, he'd been abducted by the government for criticising it for doing nothing to get people off the streets. He'd become one of the Lost.

It sounded daft to Joe, why couldn't he have just fallen into some ditch? True, his body had never been found, but that didn't mean he'd been kidnapped. Perhaps these Christians believed things like that because they needed a bit of excitement in their sad lives. When he asked his dad what he thought, he got the reply that over the years a number of people had vanished without trace, dozens of them, all people who'd been critical of the powers that be and wouldn't shut up. Joe asked why people weren't kicking up a fuss and was told that they were afraid of becoming 'Lost' too.

Sure, thought Joe, some people may have disappeared – perhaps they'd become stressed out, couldn't face their responsibilities, so they'd made themselves homeless or gone off to South America. The numbers had been added to and the stories made more mysterious by the fantasy-lovers who spread them – like people in the last century who said they'd seen flying saucers. Pathetic.

But he didn't think that way now. For now it was happening to them. It all fitted. That was why they'd wanted the car keys, why they'd gone to collect the kayak before anyone noticed it. And that was why they weren't blindfolded, no one cared if they saw where they were going. For they wouldn't be coming back. The Lost stayed that way.

They wouldn't be coming back. That meant... *he* wouldn't be coming back. He wouldn't be going to that Shams concert with Anna, he'd never see her again in fact, or his home, his room, his mates. He'd never go in the kayak again, feel the roll of the waves under the boat… The thoughts were rushing in now… He would never go to school again, never get to take his Profession Entrance exams, never become an Internet vetter, never get married, never have kids… Never.

It was like he was… dead.

For a moment his mouth gaped in silent horror, then something inside his throat seemed to snap, and he was howling at the top of his voice, tears streaming down his face, his whole body jerking round in the seat, hands flying up and clawing at air, feet stamping on the floor of the van. He could feel his father's arms reaching out to him, but unable to grip him, unable to hold him down.

Then it was over, and he slumped in his seat, wheezing, trying to catch his breath. His father's arms encircled him and pulled him close. This time he did not resist, he didn't have the strength. After a moment, he became aware of his father's voice by his ear, whispering. At first he couldn't hear the words above his own breathing, then he did, 'God won't forget us. You'll see. God won't forget us…'

But Joe had to see that hope on his father's face, had to know it wasn't some half-believed cliché to keep him quiet. So he looked up. And his father was smiling down at him. Smiling. He really did believe it.

'Yes, Joe, it's true. It'll work out. You'll see.'

But the Vulture had heard the words as well and turned his head. Joe looked at him. He was smiling too. But it wasn't the same kind of smile: it was full of derision and perhaps pity. And Joe remembered: there was no God, so there would be no help, it wouldn't 'work out'. Ever. No matter what his father believed. Ever.

He vomited onto the shoes of the soldier opposite.

'Whoops,' said the Vulture, still smiling, and handed him a tissue.

He slept a little after that and only woke when the van stopped. The early evening sun was coming out from behind clouds now, and through the windscreen he could see massive wrought iron gates with pillars on either side. No one got out, but the gates swung slowly open and the van went through.

'Where are we, Dad?' He felt tired now.

'Some stately home by the look of it. We came through Rowfort and Saranton, then I lost track. I don't know it round here.'

Neither the Vulture nor the soldiers took any notice of their talking.

The van continued down a long avenue of trees. A large centuries-old building was just ahead, but they swung to the left, down a smaller drive that led into a wood. After a few moments they turned onto a disused path between the trees.

They came out into a grassy clearing and stopped. All the soldiers got out. The Vulture came to the back of the van.

'Please – Mr Collins.'

Joe followed his father out. He was not shaking now, just so tired that he felt dizzy. Dusk was closing in, and the dim light, together with his tiredness, made everything seem slightly blurred. He blinked his eyes to clear them and looked round.

He had been expecting a building of some kind, but it was just a space circled by trees. There were no other people there. Just Joe and his dad, the Vulture, and the soldiers, one of whom was drumming his fingers on his belt, very close to the butt of his gun…

With a burst of fear, Joe understood. The soldiers were a firing squad. The clearing had been chosen so the executions would go unheard and unseen.

The trees were still.

Everything was silent.

Then the Vulture spoke, softly, 'This way, Mr Collins.' He began walking towards the centre of the clearing.

Why don't they just shoot us now? Joe thought. He glanced across at the soldier who had looked so guilty before. Now he was as blank faced as the others.

'Mr Collins. If you please…'

Joe and his dad began moving, aware the soldiers were following. The end must be near now.

But then Joe saw he'd been wrong about the clearing being empty. There was something there: a small curved green wall, about two metres high… no, not a wall, for it curved all the way round, like a huge barrel. It went into the ground, maybe a pipe or chimney.

But he had no time to think what it could be for. For now he began to make out something else – a slot cut into the ground in front of them. Like a grave, a long grave. So this was the place.

'Stop there. Wait,' said the Vulture as they came to the edge.

And Joe saw it wasn't a grave at all. For there were steps – a stone staircase, leading down into the earth. He could just make out a door at the bottom. Like the chimney a little further on, both door and steps had been painted in shades of green. That was why they'd been difficult to see.

The Vulture took a phone from his pocket and mumbled something into it.

The door slid open. Slowly. A dim light oozed out. Joe gazed at it. What was down there? Who was down there? What were they going to do? Surely it must be better than what he'd *thought* was going to happen? Or maybe it still was going to happen.

'Please,' murmured the Vulture, waving his hand towards the door. Joe could sense the soldiers closing up behind. He knew if they didn't go down the steps by themselves, they'd be helped.

But his dad just stood there and looked at the Vulture. 'What is this place?' he demanded. It was a shock to hear such a loud voice in the silent clearing. 'Why have we not been taken to a police station? And you have not arrested my son, so why is he still here? You said—'

'Mr Collins.' Sharp, edgy. 'Not now. They are waiting for you. They will explain.'

The soldiers, as if obeying some unspoken command, took a step nearer.

Joe could see the desperation in his father's eyes. It's hopeless, Dad, he wanted to say, we both know they'll never release me now. He stood for one last moment and looked at the trees, the sky, the wispy clouds. Then he looked at the Vulture.

The Vulture met his stare and began to speak. 'I'm…' Then he lowered his eyes and stood silent.

There was nothing else to do but follow his father down the steps and through the door.

3

It was a small room lit by a neon strip. A police officer stood on the other side of a metal table, two guards in grey uniforms by a door in the left hand wall. Otherwise the room was bare. As soon as Joe and his father were inside, both guards touched a button on their belts and the door to the outside world slid shut with a metallic grinding noise and a final heavy click.

The policeman spoke, reading from a piece of paper. ''You have been arrested under Law 240 stroke 5 as a corruptor of society. You are to be held in confinement for the well-being of that society.' Do you understand what I have read to you?'

'I don't understand why my son—'

'You will be blindfolded and taken to your cell. Then the blindfold will be removed and you will be instructed in the daily routine.'

'I have asked you why—'

He got no further. One of the guards had come across with a roll of tape. He tore off a length with his teeth and silenced Joe's dad with it. And that was the last Joe saw before something was put round his head and everything went dark. The blindfold was in place.

But, unlike his dad, he did not have his mouth covered. He could still speak out, demand answers, demand their release. It's up to you now, Joe, he told himself. But fear was jamming a fist down his throat again and he said nothing.

Fingers now gripped his upper arm. 'Just walk straight ahead.' It was the policeman's voice by his ear. Then he heard that grinding noise again, but lighter this time, and he was pushed forward, further into the darkness.

And he remembered how, years before, another policeman's hand had gripped his arm like this. It was the day his mother died. Six years ago. But he could still remember every detail.

Joe loved the Leader's Day Parade. The previous year's one was still vivid in his mind. This year his parents had taken him to the corner of First Street and Green Road in such good time that they'd got a place right on the pavement edge. It was a long wait for a lad of eight and he had become a bit sulky and irritable. But when the procession came he was transported to another world.

The floats depicted the most important events in Britain since the Leader had become head of the government in 2009. The first float held just one figure – a five-metre-tall computer controlled model of the Leader waving at the crowd just as he had done at his moment of triumph all those years ago. Other floats were filled with smaller computer controlled or holographic figures, acting out the day a freak tornado threatened the Kent coast, or the time a bomb blew up part of the Tower of London, or the building of the The Leader's Hospital, the largest hospital in the world at that time.

Each float showed the Leader at the centre, making

it clear that, even though he might not have been personally present, he was still the force behind all the good work. Most people didn't think it odd that he could be seen laying bricks or pulling people out of ruined buildings. Joe had heard enough sentences that began, 'If it hadn't been for the Leader—' that he accepted him as a great hero, perhaps the greatest ever.

An identical procession took place on Leader's Day in each of the major towns in England and a special museum had been built outside each of the towns to house the floats. Joe's school had gone to its local museum a few months before and learnt how the floats were made and how the latest advances in electronics were used to update them. However, no one was allowed to see the new floats until the day of the parade.

It was while one of the new floats was passing that it happened.

The float was extraordinary, better than anything he remembered from the year before. It showed how the Leader had restored animal habitats by planting millions of trees, hedgerows and so on. There was the Leader, several times life-size, with all these computer controlled animals scampering round him and birds flying over him, landing on a shoulder for a few seconds, then flying off again. A swallow, more like an eagle in size, swooped over Joe's head before flying back to the float.

Joe screamed with surprise and fright, but Mum bent down to reassure him that the bird would be programmed not to touch anyone, and that it was far safer than any real bird.

'I know that really,' Joe said, 'but it came so close!'

They were the last words he would say to his mother.

For a little group of people at the back of the crowd had surged forward and Joe's mother was pushed off the kerb into the street. Policemen were standing at intervals along the route to make sure no one came near the floats. Now one rushed up and pushed Joe's mother back. She caught her heel in a drain cover and fell sideways, hitting her head on the edge of the kerb.

Immediately Joe's dad was there, bending over her, while Joe just stood staring, unable to take it in. Then he caught sight of his dad's face looking strange and grey and heard him murmur, 'She's dead.' But she couldn't be that, Joe knew, because she'd just fallen over.

Suddenly he felt fingers gripping his arm. The policeman's face was close to his. He could see him sweating, smell something metallic on his breath like he'd been sucking coins. And he could hear his words, 'I never pushed your mum, you know that, don't you?' But Joe didn't know that, he just knew his mother was lying in the gutter and that he needed to see what was wrong. He pulled away from the policeman and knelt with his father who was now cradling his wife in his arms and sobbing loudly.

And Joe was sobbing, because his mother was hurt and because he'd wet himself and because everywhere around were shocked faces and people were patting him. And because the procession was going by and he couldn't see it through his tears.

Strangers came to the house a few days later, a man with a slit of a mouth, like he'd shaved off his lips by mistake (Joe knew about shaving: when his father had finished, he sometimes ran the shaver over Joe's chin, it felt hot and tickly) and a woman who kept giving Joe little smiles which he felt was stupid.

They sat with Joe and his dad, asked how they were, how they felt about what had happened, about the policeman, about the Leader. They looked round. The woman picked up the Bible from his father's desk, flicked through it, put it down again. The man looked at the titles in the bookcase.

Then they went. Joe was glad.

But the memory of their faces did not go, and several years later when Lips-shaved-off appeared on the Internet news – he was walking beside the Leader – Joe recognised him instantly. 'Dad, look, that man, after Mum died, remember? Dad, why did they come?' Joe had never asked before, he had never wanted to know.

'It was to make sure I still loved the Leader and his police force. Do you remember, Joe, last year, that man Adam Hutton was arrested for planting bombs by statues of the Leader? It turned out that some time before, one of the Leader's bodyguards had frightened his little daughter while they were queuing to see the Leader's home. Just a little thing but it triggered off a hostility towards anything to do with the Leader. They came to make sure I wasn't another rebel in the making, that I didn't blame the powers that be for your mother's death. They probably keep an eye on me even now in case I turn bitter and twisted.'

'But it would be wrong to blame the Leader for any of that about Mum. The Leader's great, he's done so much good.'

'Yes, Joe, he has, but keep an open mind. There are

some things—'

'Dad—'

'Oh, I know what they teach you at school, Joe. And I know you're supposed to tell your teacher if I give you wrong ideas about the Leader. I'm just saying learn to think for yourself.'

'I am. And I think he's great. All right?' Joe was getting angry now, and afraid. He didn't like it when his dad said things against the Leader. He needed them both to be on the same side.

Joe began to walk. He had no choice with the policeman gripping his arm.

Through that side door. Into a passage or another room, impossible to tell. It smelt strange, antiseptic.

Steered to the right. A few steps, right again.

A whirring noise. A door sliding open.

Several more steps. Then harder pressure on his arm. The man was turning him to face the way he'd come. What was happening? Were they going back again?

The door slid shut.

A moment of panic forced the words out. 'Dad, are you there?'

A muffled grunt. Yes, he was there. They were still together.

Then the world fell away under his feet.

Of course. A lift.

It seemed to go on and on.

Finally it shuddered to a stop and the door slid open. Walking again, slightly to the right this time, about ten paces.

'Lift up your foot. There's a step here.'

He could feel his heel on the edge as he put his foot down again. Then his arm was released and he could feel the ends of the blindfold being pulled apart. He could see. His father was next to him, having the tape peeled from his mouth.

Joe looked around. A small room, narrow. Ceiling, walls and floor all pale blue, a kind of plastic. Two beds set along the sides of the room, opposite each other: not beds though, more like boxes – long boxes, moulded to the walls and floor, same colour, same material. There was a white mattress and a pile of folded bedding on each bed.

The policeman and one of the guards were just inside the doorway. The other one was standing in the centre of the room. He cleared his throat and pointed to a tiny grating above the door. 'Air here,' he said. 'The heat is controlled.'

Then to the corner to the right of the door. Another pale blue box moulded to floor and walls with a pile of toilet rolls to one side. 'Toilet here. Inside, bucket with lid.'

Next up to the neon strip embedded in the ceiling. 'Light. Goes dim at night.'

Then finally beyond the beds to the short wall opposite the door. 'Your food, everything you need comes here.' Joe could just make out a recessed hatch running almost the length of the wall, with a small round handle at the right hand end. 'When food comes, bell rings. You have thirty seconds to take out food containers, washing water, things like that, and new toilet bucket. You must put used one in its place. Food will come three times a day, the other things twice. All clean clothes tomorrow, then you get clean underwear, things like that, twice a week. I think, on this lift, it's Sundays and Wednesdays. Bedclothes once a week. Also there is microphone in lift if trouble or ill. Understand?'

The man had an accent but Joe could understand the words all right. But he didn't understand what they meant. They didn't make sense. He knew what prisons were like and they weren't like this. They had dining halls and rooms where you could have visitors and places to exercise.

Then the policeman and guards went back through the doorway, both guards again touching a button in their belts. The door slid shut with a whine. There was no handle and no lock. Joe could just make out the rectangular slit in the plastic.

He looked across at his father. Dazed like him. He sat on the edge of the bed, looked around. But there was nothing else to see.

'Is this it?' he murmured.

His father sighed. 'I don't believe it. I thought we'd be taken to some ordinary prison, just kept away from the other prisoners. But this is new, Joe. This must have been built just for the Lost.'

'So what happens now?'

And he saw the answer on his father's face. Nothing happens now. From today this was all there was.

4

They sat in silence.

Finally, Joe couldn't stop his feelings spilling out. He glared at his father as he spat out the words. 'It's your fault, all of this. If it wasn't for you, we wouldn't be here. It's all your Christian stuff that's got us into this, you just went on and on with it. Didn't you ever think of me while you were doing it, didn't you ever think that I wanted a life? You know I wanted to work at the Internet Centre! That's all gone, all gone!'

He knew he was getting louder and louder, almost shrieking, but couldn't stop, like the crying in the van, couldn't help it.

'Now what have I got to look forward to? Nothing! Nothing! Just cooped up here with you! And I haven't done anything, in fact I hate those stupid comics you draw, hate them!'

His father just looked at him sadly.

'Just don't tell me any of that 'God won't forget us' rubbish – not now, not ever! I hate God and I hate you! And now I'm stuck here with—'

He couldn't get any more words out. He just sat on the edge of the bed and tried to catch his breath.

Quietly his father came across, moved the blankets to one side and sat by his son. Without looking up at him, Joe leant against him and allowed himself to be held close and rocked gently. After a few moments the tears came, rolling down his face and into his father's lap.

No food or drink came that evening. They were halfway through tucking the blankets around the thin mattress when the light dimmed.

But they didn't talk about it.

'Goodnight, Joe,' was all his father said. Joe didn't answer – what was the point? He just took off his trainers and pulled the bedclothes around him.

When he woke the full light was on again. His father was dressed and sitting on his bed.

'How did you sleep, Joe?'

Before he went to sleep, he'd vowed he wouldn't speak to his father again to punish him. But now he couldn't stop himself saying, 'All right.'

His father smiled. 'Good. Listen, can you hear that noise?'

'No, what noise? Oh yes, behind the hatch.' A humming noise, interrupted by an occasional clanking sound and in the distance... was that a doorbell? 'The lift with the food?'

'Yes, but it's been going some time. That must mean there are other people here, a lot of them probably.'

'Maybe Dan's brother.' Dan was the pastor of his dad's church.

'Yes, I thought of him. I wonder if there's any way we can send messages?'

'Tapping on the walls?' Joe was surprised at how

soon his anger had dropped away. He knew in his heart his father would have done anything to keep him from this: he remembered his words on the beach had been 'Sorry, Joe', and every word after that had been about getting him released. He couldn't have known they would come for him like that, certainly not come when Joe was around.

A bell rang behind the hatch.

Joe's father jumped up and pulled at the handle. The hatch door slid to the left, folding concertina-like into a bracket just behind the wall. Slotted into holders in the lift's base, which was at waist level, were a number of plastic tubs of different sizes and colours. Clothes and other items were heaped on one side.

'Help me take this lot out. I'll change the toilet bucket.'

They had just placed everything on the cell floor when the bell rang again. They looked at the open hatch. The bell rang again and again. What were they supposed to do now?

Joe thought of it first. 'We've got to close the hatch, Dad.' He slid it along until it clipped shut. The bell stopped and they could hear the lift moving again.

They looked at everything they'd received: apart from the containers there were towels and flannels, wrapped soap, toothbrush and paste, bottles of drinking water with mugs and another roll of toilet paper to go with the pile they already had.

'They must think we spent the night on the loo.'

'I think, Joe, some people on the first night do just that. Out of sheer fright. Can you imagine how it would have been if they'd split us up? I praise God they didn't.'

Joe hadn't thought of that. Being alone in here – he couldn't have stood it, just couldn't. He opened one of the two largest tubs. 'Phew, the smell! What's this? Soup for breakfast?'

'Joe, that's not soup. It's the water to wash in, you nit. I'm glad it's hot, I'm feeling grubby. Shall we do that first?'

The water had a disinfectant in it. It was the smell Joe had noticed upstairs. He wondered if it would bring him out in spots and for a second he thought about how Anna wouldn't even look at him if that happened. Then he realised what a stupid thought that was. Anna wouldn't be looking at him at all from now on. Quickly, before he had time to take it in properly, he began sorting through the clothes. When the guard had said about clean clothes, he'd imagined some kind of prison uniform, but this was just cheap, ordinary stuff – thin jeans, denim shirts, chain store underwear and socks. Then he noticed that, written with a marker pen on each of the shirt labels, there were two initials: AC on one, JC on the other. He glanced through: everything was marked AC or JC.

JC. His initials. It was like a punch in the face. JC: this is his wardrobe. From now on he'd never get to choose anything. Someone else would choose and they'd always choose cheap and nasty. He sighed. What was the point of worrying about how you looked down here? At least it was all new, it would have been horrible if they'd come off some dead prisoner. And it'd be good to get out of his sweaty T-shirt and shorts. He sorted them into JC and AC, then washed quickly.

'Well, mine fit,' said his dad. 'One of the guards must be used to sizing people up. Yours?'

'Yeah. What happens to our own stuff? Keep it here with us?'

'It's going to smell, Joe. I reckon the lift will come again for the empties. Send it up then. And I should wear the belt. The next pair they send may be too big and we don't want to go around holding our trousers up.'

Go around? Go around where exactly? But he did not argue, just retrieved the belt from under his dirty clothes and mumbled, 'Not a proper belt anyway, just a tacky little strip of plastic,' and put it on. Then he turned to the other tubs and lifted the lids. 'Porridge, tea, halves of toast, cold.'

'Probably the job of the night staff to make the toast.'

'And I can't stand porridge.'

'Somehow, Joe, I don't think they're too worried about that.' He bowed his head and said thanks in a murmur. Joe was used to that and just stared into his porridge until his father said, 'Right, let's start.'

Not long after the lift had collected the containers and the dirty clothes, the door of the cell slid open and the same two guards came in.

'Now,' announced the one who had spoken before, 'I give haircuts.' He was holding a battery shaver. 'Sit down, please.' He pointed Joe's dad to the bed.

'And if we don't want our hair cut?'

The guard looked puzzled. 'You missed round. Two days ago. So I do now.'

'I guess if I say no, you'd stick tape on me and do it anyway.'

The razor skimmed over his scalp, every few

seconds the guard emptying the cut hair from the shaver into a plastic bag held by his colleague. Then it was Joe's turn. He couldn't be bothered to object. His hair was short anyway, it only took a minute. Then they all watched the second guard carefully tie a knot to seal the bag.

'Special bucket will come once a week for washing hair. Understand?'

Without waiting for an answer, they left the cell and the doorway disappeared.

Joe looked at his dad. 'Hey, Dad, you look okay. Different – but okay. Your bald spot doesn't show up so much.' His father smiled. And Joe realised he'd smiled too.

When the whirring began again they listened carefully and could make out each time the lift stopped. They counted them. It made five stops before their own bell rang. When they'd shut the door they carried on listening. One more stop below, and that was it.

Over lunch (pasta with a thin tomato sauce, stewed apples), Joe's dad said, 'So. Seven cells vertically, but did you notice those sounds as we unloaded? More than one lift, do you think?'

Joe nodded. 'Remember how the guard said something like, 'On *this* lift the clothes come Sundays and Wednesdays,' so, yeah, there must be more than one. I reckon by the sound of them there's – what? Six, do you think? That would mean six cells on each floor.'

'And most of them occupied.'

'Two to a cell, you reckon?'

'Probably, Joe. Why send the lifts on more journeys than they need?'

It was as they were putting the lids back on the containers that Joe said quietly, 'So, Dad, why should God remember us when he seems to have forgotten about all these others?'

His father sighed. 'I can't answer that, Joe. I just know that God is faithful and he won't let us down.'

'Yeah.' Joe couldn't be bothered to argue. How could he if his dad ignored all the facts? Joe knew what the evidence said. There is no God. Full stop. He remembered the day he'd decided to go with the evidence even though it meant going against Dad. The turning point. Two years ago. It had seemed an ordinary school day until he was called up to talk to the teacher.

He'd always loved school, right from when his mother had taken him for the official 'look round' day.

'Now, Joe, there's going to be a lot of big boys and girls there, but I'll be with you, so don't worry.'

But Joe wasn't worried. He was almost six after all. In the last few months he'd grown impatient with pre-school playing about, tired of being treated like a baby. He couldn't wait to move on, and because he was an only child with no older brother or sister to dispel the mysteries of real school, that visit was like entering a magic kingdom. It wasn't the size of the school or the children which made it magic: it was the machinery.

Even in School 1, he now learnt, he'd have a mini computer on top of his desk all the time, and no one would be saying, 'It's my turn to use it now, Joe,' like they did at home.

In School 2, which he'd reach in three years' time, it was even better. Not that it appeared that way at first.

In fact, when his mother led him into the School 2 classroom she said, 'Strange, it looks like a classroom from generations ago, desks in rows and all facing front.'

But, after all the parents and children had crammed in, the teacher explained that when the desks were opened, they revealed computers with the screen in the desk lid. 'This is the very latest equipment, and it's constantly being updated. Pupils have access to many more web sites than you have at home, including of course those specially created by the school. These are of a far higher standard than anything available outside. In the lid of my desk I have a master screen which enables me to see what each child is working on and I can call up any of their screens onto the large wall screen here at the front so we can go through it together. I assure you, our resources are the very best and when your children arrive in School 2, the quality will be even better.'

Wow, thought Joe.

Those three years of School 1 passed quickly. When his parents, then later just his father, came for the regular parents' evenings, they were always told the same story: 'Joe is a talented child, a quick thinker, full of initiative. We've great hopes for him in Schools 2 and 3.'

Then he was there, in that same School 2 classroom he'd seen with his mother.

But it was hard work. Monday to Thursday mornings were carefully monitored. Subject sheets with names of appropriate web sites were passed round each day, Joe always receiving the top-level sheets.

The task was usually to find out all he could about one area of knowledge and make written notes, then sort them out to make an interesting printout. He seemed to have natural ability for Computer Aided Design, and he was a fast typist. Often the teacher would bring up onto the front screen a web site Joe had found that wasn't on the school list, or would use Joe's final result as a model for what could be done.

The five afternoons were given over to art and craft work, which Joe hated, and PSA (Physical and Social Activities), which he loved. Just a few years before, the Leader had announced 'sweeping changes in education': schools should offer, he said, more challenging activities. 'Challenging physically and challenging socially: just running round a track or getting a ball through a net is not enough'. So PSA was born, and every School 2 and School 3 had to provide facilities for abseiling, rock climbing and emergency training.

Emergency training was fun. It was done in groups and could be anything from making a waterproof tent to constructing a stretcher to carry an injured person, always using the most ridiculous materials to make it 'challenging'. But the other two activities were more than just fun. For Joe, they were seriously exciting.

His school, which was an 'All-Ager' with Schools 1, 2 and 3 on the same site, was only two storeys high. There was no wall suitable for abseiling down so one had to be built on the school field. Three sections of a mountain face for rock climbing were also built: a section you could walk up with a bit of help from the tutor at the top holding the rope, one with steep parts where you'd have to search for finger- and toe-holds, and one reserved for School 3 with a nasty overhang and a chimney. Joe bit his lip with fear when he saw all this going up – he was terrified of heights. But as soon as he started, the sheer thrill of being far above the ground took over, allowing him to achieve success where he'd least expected it.

At various points around the school, there were huge photos of the Leader – holding an abseiler's rope or joining in some piece of emergency training – to remind pupils whom they should thank for all the fun and excitement they were having. But Joe, like all pupils, knew that anyway. He knew it from day one in School 1 when he'd been taught the Saying – words that had to be recited by pupils, even teachers, at the start of the day in all schools. They had to stand to attention before the Flag and chant, 'Help me to be faithful to my country, its Leader and ministers. Make me a good citizen, honest and true, hardworking and thankful, today and every day. So be it.' It sounded to Joe a bit like one of the prayers at church, although of course there was no mention of God in it (there was no religious instruction at school and God was never mentioned). Joe never wondered whose help he was asking for in the Saying.

On Friday mornings, pupils could work on individual projects. Joe loved surfing the Net, trying to come up with bizarre bits of information he could include. 'Changes in Popular Music in the 21st Century' in his final year in School 2 was his favourite project so far and he would spend hours delving into unofficial web sites on the Shams or the Bloomen or Razzy B. Then the deceptively gentle tones of his teacher, Mr Webb, would come drifting across the room, 'Joe Collins, may I ask, are you using your time in absolutely the most profitable way? Mmm?' And Joe would change sites quickly.

But he was making really good progress on the Friday morning it happened. Mr Webb had praised him on it. 'The way you're putting it together, Joe, I could almost become interested in pop music myself. Almost.' So he reckoned he could take a breather and investigate something that had nothing to do with his project and Mr Webb would turn a blind eye. The Sunday before, a man had come to the church and asked for prayer for his country, where there were many Christians in prison for their faith. This man had emigrated to the States when he was young, and now he felt he owed it to his countrymen to travel the world telling churches about the situation. 'Some have been tortured and killed just because they wanted to be faithful to Jesus.' Joe could hardly believe anyone would prefer to suffer, even die, than give up their religion. Anyway, why couldn't they just say, 'Yeah, all right, I'll give it up,' but secretly go on believing? Crazy.

But Joe couldn't stop thinking about it. Was the man making it up? Did it happen in other countries too? His father didn't know much more so he tried to get some information off the Net at home. There were many sites on prisoners open to him, but as soon as he went for information on Christian prisoners the screen went blank. The web sites had been blocked. Why? He knew the government blocked access to sites which 'threatened security or moral well-being' as they put it, but what was so harmful about a group of prisoners on the other side of the world?

He knew the school was allowed access to some of these blocked sites: in School 3 they studied some controversial subjects so, under the eye of the teacher, selected sites were opened up for viewing and discussion. Could he access them in School 2 he wondered. He typed up the key words. Yes! Here they came. Some sites had a person's name as the title, some a country, some an organisation that was trying to help. He searched for the country the speaker had come from. Yes, there it all was, just as he'd said, and here there were prisoners' names and other details. He tried another country's site and found out churches had been burnt down, Bibles destroyed, Christians beaten. So why did they go on believing in a God who didn't—

'Joe, may I see you for a moment, please?'

Joe looked up. He'd been so immersed in the sites, he'd forgotten where he was or what he should be doing. 'Sorry, Mr Webb, I'll get on now.'

'Could you come here, please?'

He went across.

'Joe, why were you looking at those sites?' His voice was soft, friendly.

'We had someone come to our church—'

'Didn't you realise those sites are for the classes on Politics in School 3?'

'Ah. Right. But I was really interested—'

'Oh, I could see you were interested, Joe. May I make a suggestion?'

Joe couldn't understand the tone. He wasn't sure if he was being told off or not. 'Er, yes.'

'Joe, you're an excellent student. What do you want to do for a career? Had you thought about that?'

Joe smiled. 'Yes, Mr Webb. I want to work for the

Government Internet Programme.'

'Yes, I wondered if it was something like that. It's a great job, Joe. Not easy to get in though. It takes commitment.'

'Yes, I know. I—'

'Commitment, Joe. So you must be careful. You know that your computer keeps a record of the sites you visit. If the government were to study your list and find too many sites on religion, and if they heard that you went to church regularly and that you were 'really interested' – your words, Joe – in people who took their religion too seriously, well, they may think that you were not totally committed to the Leader. Divided loyalties, they may think.'

'Well, it's just that my dad goes to church, so I—'

'Joe, it's up to you. But my advice would be to decide where your loyalties lie. I've seen people, Joe, get so mixed up with the old superstitions that they throw away their opportunities. Do you get my meaning?'

Joe got his meaning. There was a decision to be made.

And he made it.

'I didn't know it would look like that. Of course I... But I can't just suddenly stop going to church.'

'No, not all at once. I understand that. But I think you need to show between now and your Profession Entrance exams that you are committed 100 per cent to the Leader.'

'But I am committed to the Leader, I am. I—'

'Thank you, Joe. Go back to your seat now.'

'What are you thinking about, Joe?'

Joe looked up with a start. 'School.'

His father nodded. 'Well, let's stack this lot ready. When the lift comes down next time, I want to use the mike. I've been thinking about all those people using the same lift. I've got an idea.'

They had their words ready. Joe flicked the switch on the mike box and waited for his father to speak first.

'This is Andrew Collins. I would like a Bible, a notebook and some pencils, please.'

'And I'd like a personal stereo with Shams and Bloomen CDs. Please.'

After the lift had gone Joe said, 'Do you really think we'll get any of that?' His father shrugged. 'And where are we going to put these notes, did you say?'

'There's a tiny gap between the bottom ring that holds the wash bucket and the base of the lift. I'm banking on whoever fills the lift being too busy to notice and the next prisoner on the list not being too busy. I don't know what will come of it, but we could get some idea of who's in here. And maybe some idea of what we can do about getting out.'

Joe glanced up at his dad. Hadn't he grasped it? He couldn't *do* anything.

His father caught his look. 'Joe, you've got to believe it. God's got a plan.'

Yeah, he thought, the same one he had for all those Christians in prison in other parts of the world. He could still remember that man coming to the church and asking for prayer, but he couldn't remember him coming back and saying, thanks for the prayers, they're all free now. Because they weren't.

No, there was no plan. There couldn't be. For there was no God.

5

The nightmares began that night. Joe was lying in a long box. He could see daylight round the edge of the lid. Then shovelfuls of earth began pouring down, blocking out the light. Suddenly, he realised – he was in a coffin. But he couldn't be, that didn't make sense – he wasn't dead. Didn't they know that? He pounded on the lid, shouted out, 'I'm alive, I'm alive!' But they couldn't seem to hear him. There was so much earth on the lid now that it was sinking and Joe could feel it pressing on his face, squashing it. He couldn't move, couldn't breathe.

He woke up screaming.

He lay on his bed the next day, only moving to eat and go to the toilet. When his father spoke to him, he just mumbled 'yes' or 'no' or said nothing. None of the things they'd asked for arrived.

It was worse the next night. The same dream, but it carried on, unstoppable. Now the coffin lid was breaking under the weight of the earth, and the earth, cold and dry, began to dribble through the cracks, scampering like tiny insects over his face, covering his eyes, blocking his nose, pushing through his lips till his cheeks bulged with it. He clamped his lips together, but it was too late. He'd have to swallow, have to—

Then hands were circling him, lifting him up and the earth was spilling out of him. So much earth, pouring out, leaving him empty and clean. He could breathe.

His father was still holding him when the light came on.

Nothing arrived that day either. He didn't speak at all now. It was too much effort.

The third night something came that was worse than earth. He was back in the coffin and the earth was seeping in again, but he could handle that: he pressed his teeth together, his lips together, he'd be safe this time. But there were things moving in the earth. He could feel them on his chest, his arms. They were beginning to move up towards his face, masses of them.

Worms! He could feel their slimy chill as they pushed against his skin to work themselves up. No! They mustn't reach his face! Suddenly his arms, which had been pinned to his side, came free and he lunged up and began peeling them off his chest, then his neck. He made his arms move faster, faster, grabbing handfuls of them. But they were multiplying all the time. Some were on his chin now. If only he could see them. He struggled to open his eyes, but the weight of the earth on the lids made it so difficult. He began shaking his head, faster, faster.

Then, suddenly, his eyes were open. And he saw his father kneeling beside him, gazing up at the ceiling of the cell, his whole body trembling, sweat running down his face. He was shouting out, but the words were hard to hear. Joe could only make out, 'Please, God!' repeated again and again. He didn't seem to be aware that Joe was looking at him.

Then Joe felt his eyes grow heavy again and before he could say anything he fell back into the darkness.

But it was all right now. The worms had gone and there was no earth pressing down on him. He felt weightless, free. He slept.

When he woke he knew it was morning for the light was full on. He looked across at his father, still asleep. He looked awful, the skin of his face white and stretched like an old man's. How long had he been praying over him? Had the prayers worked then? But how could they work when no one was listening? Or had his father radiated some power which had reached into Joe's mind?

Joe sat on his bed looking at him. He didn't know what to think.

Then his father blinked open his eyes, saw Joe, and smiled.

They had a surprise when they opened the lift door. A Bible – a paperback, but a new one. Personal hi-fi with two Shams CDs, one Bloomen. But nothing to write with or on.

'I think they realised what we wanted it for,' said his dad. 'Perhaps everybody stuck in here thinks of it. They don't care what we read or listen to, they just don't want us to communicate. Of course, that's why they collect the dirty dishes one cell at a time.'

'Dad, you could tear out separate words from the Bible, make a message that way.'

'Good idea, but they'd see it straight off.'

'Perhaps we could ask for a Net chat room to be set up between cells.'

'You would think of that!'

Joe grinned back.

He settled back on his bed and put on the headphones. For a couple of hours he almost forgot where he was.

'Do I get a go then?'

'Dad, I know you've got a supercool haircut for the first time in your life, but you might still be a bit, er, well, old for the Shams.'

'I know I couldn't stand their stuff before, but there's not much to choose from now, is there? Come on, let's hear it.'

Joe looked at his dad's face while he listened.

'Yeah, the haircut must have altered my brain cells. It seemed okay. I couldn't understand a word though.'

Joe smiled. 'Probably as well, Dad.' His father looked better now, the music had relaxed him a bit. Neither of them had mentioned what had happened in the night.

Then his dad said, 'So what about reading a bit of the Bible now?'

For a moment Joe felt hurt. Was that the idea then? I'll show an interest in your stupid music so you'll feel you have to show an interest in the Bible? No, that was unfair, his dad wasn't like that. He wanted to share his present, that was all. Just a shame it was such a useless present. Joe couldn't remember much of the Bible from his churchgoing days, but he was pretty sure there was nothing relevant to a life spent locked in a cell. He shrugged. 'If you like.'

'What about a psalm? The writers often had a rough time. David wrote many of them, you know, the shepherd boy who became a king—'

Just what he'd thought – totally irrelevant. 'Dad, shepherds wander over hills, kings live in palaces – they're buildings with doors that open. I wouldn't mind a rough time like that.'

His father didn't react to the sarcasm, just nodded and said, 'Okay, what about your namesake, Joseph?'

Joe shrugged again. It didn't matter. 'I guess.'

But it was good to hear his dad read, it reminded him of how he would read Joe off to sleep every night after Mum died. Sometimes it would take a long time, but Dad had just kept on reading.

' "Jacob loved Joseph more than all his other sons, because he had been born to him when he was old. He made a long robe with full sleeves for him. When his brothers saw that their father loved Joseph more than he loved them, they hated their brother so much that they would not speak to him in a friendly manner." '

Well, that's one good thing about being an only child, thought Joe, you don't have any of that to put up with.

' "One night Joseph had a dream, and when he told his brothers about it, they hated him even more. He said, 'Listen to the dream I had. We were all in the field tying up sheaves of wheat, when my sheaf got up and stood up straight. Yours formed a circle round mine and bowed down to it.' " '

Joe sighed. Not the brightest, my namesake, he thought, even I would have had the sense to keep that dream quiet. But he could see the similarity between himself and the Joseph of the Bible, for when it came down to it, he'd seen his future in the same way – above his fellows, with them bowing to his decisions.

' "So Joseph went after his brothers and found them at Dothan. They saw him in the distance and before he reached them, they plotted against him and decided to kill him. They said to one another, 'Come on now, let's kill him and throw his body into one of the dry wells.' When Joseph came up to his brothers, they ripped off his long robe with full sleeves. Then they took him and threw him into the well." '

And Joe remembered when, with his dad, he'd been thrown into this 'well', deep in the earth.

' "...and when some traders came by, the brothers pulled Joseph out of the well and sold him for twenty pieces of silver to the Ishmaelites, who took him to Egypt." '

His dad looked up and smiled. 'At least we weren't dragged in here behind a camel!'

Joe nodded half-heartedly. He didn't feel like jokes. Anyway, he hadn't been thinking of that side of it. He'd been thinking about how Joseph's dreams had exploded in his face. One moment he had a great future to look forward to, the next – no future at all.

And that was something Joe could relate to.

The letter had arrived a week before his fourteenth birthday.

He had left School 2 now but he hadn't forgotten that conversation with Mr Webb. Nor had he forgotten a second conversation that same day when he got home from school, this time with his father. Joe had wanted to get it over with straight away. 'I've been thinking, Dad. I'm not sure I've got the time to go to church every week now. I mean, just at the moment, like. I mean, I can come some weeks, but I'm getting more and more schoolwork, and I really want to do my best. Do you see what I mean, Dad?'

But he could tell his father didn't see what he meant at all and he braced himself for a lecture on honouring God. Whatever his dad said though, he wasn't going to change his mind and he certainly wasn't going to tell him what had brought on this sudden eagerness for schoolwork. That understanding with Mr Webb was going to remain his little secret.

The lecture never came though, nor did his father ask why. He just nodded, said he would miss his company at church, but when he wanted to go, just say. It was all very quiet.

Joe wondered if his relief was a bit too obvious. He'd even been scared his dad would march into school and tell them they were overworking his son. If he'd seen Mr Webb, Joe's decision could so easily have come out in the open.

It was a decision he was determined to stick to. The decision not to believe. He had so much to gain.

So he went to church every other week for a couple of months, then once a month, then not at all. Easy. Now he was free. Free to get where he wanted.

And the arrival of the letter proved he'd done the right thing.

Selected School 3s had been asked for the names of two pupils who might be suitable for working for the Programme, not just ones who liked surfing the Net but ones who'd shown initiative and, of course, commitment to the Leader. They were to be taken to the Programme's headquarters in Guildford and given a guided tour. Joe's school was one of the selected ones but he didn't dare think about it too much. There were older kids who were more advanced than he was.

When he opened the envelope and saw the sheet headed with the Leader's name and official address, he didn't connect it with the Programme, couldn't think what it was about – was he in trouble? He tried to read it through but his eyes kept jumping from line to line and he couldn't get the sense of it. It was only when his dad took the sheet from his trembling fingers and read it aloud that he understood.

'Well, congratulations, Joe, that'll be one exciting day. You must be making quite an impression at school.'

Joe grinned, shrugged. Could this have anything to do with Mr Webb, with that conversation? He glanced up, caught the look on his father's face. He looked stunned.

For they both knew that it wasn't just an invitation to a day out; it was saying: keep on in the same way, and there could be a career waiting here for you with all its privileges: huge salary, automatic tickets for sporting events, priority parking everywhere – and the pleasure and security of being one of the Chosen Ones. Of course Joe knew there were only so many posts available, and there'd be plenty of School 3s sending their best pupils, but even so. Wow – on the Leader's official notepaper too.

He became aware that his father was talking, '...but you'll have to think, Joe, even if it did work out, if it's really what you want to do. There are so many options

– university, travelling the world, and you've got nearly four years left in School 3 yet. Don't let yourself be sucked into—'

Joe couldn't stop himself. He knew, just knew, his father would say something like that. He was so biased against the Leader, so out of touch. 'I'm not getting sucked into anything. Don't spoil it for me, okay?' And he snatched the letter back and strode past him to his own room.

He slammed the door, knelt by the bed and tried in vain to smooth out the crumpled sheet of paper.

'Hi. I'm Ricky and I'm your guide for your day's visit to the Programme. We're very proud of the Centre, it's one of only five in the world, and the only one in Europe. Other countries don't seem to care what their people read on the Net. But our Leader cares. And we here put that care into action.' He looked down at his clipboard. 'It's schools from Kent and Sussex here today, I think… yes, great. But let me tell you straight off, you're not just visitors today, you're workers. We'll be giving you some real experience in decision making – I hope you're up to it!'

Joe gazed at Ricky. He was everything Joe wanted to be – in looks, style, confidence – and position. Hi, I'm Joe, I'm your guide for today… yeah, it sounded good. He looked round at the group, wondered how many of them were putting their own names in the same sentence. Yes, plenty of competition, but there'd be plenty of that just to become the guy who cleaned the floor.

'First up, I'm going to take you to the Switchboard. Follow me, please.'

They went down a long corridor. At the end of it, Ricky used a keypad to open a door. 'Step inside. Careful, it's dark in here.'

It reminded Joe of a cinema. A bank of a hundred desks, probably more, each topped with a monitor, curved in semi circles facing a large screen.

'This is where we sort every new web site, as well as ones that have been updated. These folk are called Classifiers, their job is to view the first page of each site that lands on their monitor, and decide which room it should be sent to for vetting. You can see the options they have on the large screen on the wall.'

The screen was divided into panels headed 'Sports', 'Travel', 'Politics' and so on; below each heading was a cluster of red lights.

'Say the Classifier reckons the site's main subject is Travel, he presses his Travel button and a red light appears up there in the Travel panel and on a similar panel in the Travel Room itself. When a Vet in that room brings it up on his monitor, then its light goes out here. So we can see if a big backlog is building up for one subject – like there was for Sports around the time of the last Olympics. In which case, the Classifier may choose to send it to a room which is quieter, so everyone's kept busy. Why don't you take five minutes and look over a few shoulders, okay?'

* * *

'Right, let's move on to a Vet Room: shall we stick with Travel or shall we try Sports?' There was a chorus of 'Sports'. Ricky laughed. 'Yeah, I don't know why I ask, they all say that!'

Another corridor, another door sliding open. A room laid out like the Switchboard, but rather smaller.

'So there are the red lights up on the screen again. Each one, remember, represents a site sent here by the Switchboard, each one needing to be thoroughly checked. You see, even a site on football or tennis could contain something harmful. There may be some reference to Britain not having enough facilities for a particular sport or there might be bad language, so the Vetter can cancel any page or the whole site. Or he might cancel it for public viewing but keep it for schools, in which case he sends it on to the Education Room: that's where we'll go next.'

'Ricky, how many rooms are there like this?' It was a girl at the back of the group.

'About thirty – one for each of the panels on the Switchboard screen. But they're not all as big as this. There are only a couple of people in Gardening, for example. The two biggest rooms are Religion and Politics, because the Vets there have to work very slowly and carefully, we don't want any strange ideas getting through, and in Politics, of course, we must protect the Leader. It's rare for a reference to him to get through.'

'What happens if someone tries to spread lies about the Leader then?' That same girl.

'The site is cancelled, obviously, but then the Trackers may get involved. They can pinpoint exactly where the site originated.'

'So what would happen to the person who created it?'

'Well, if it's in this country, he'd be dealt with straightaway. If it's abroad, then we'd need to contact our nearest agents. Now. On to Education, okay?'

'Dealt with'? thought Joe. 'Agents'? Sounded

ominous. But it was right of course. It would be terrible if wrong information about the Leader got around. He thought how quickly even his own father would latch on to anything critical. He'd believe it, no questions asked. And it struck Joe that was the best job of all: Tracker. Like a bodyguard to the Leader, only protecting him against lies rather than bullets. Better than being a Tour Guide even.

'Here in the Education Room everyone is an expert. If a web site banned for general use arrives here, the expert in that subject will check it out. If he rates it as accurate, then it might get onto the schools register, for use only under supervision in School 3s and Universities. You've probably used a few of them.'

Joe remembered the site on Christian prisoners. What Ricky said meant it had been passed as accurate, and that those Christians really were in prison, tortured, killed. It was all true. He pushed the thought out of his mind and tuned into Ricky again.

'Now, I'm going to take you to a rest area where you can eat your lunch. This afternoon each of you will be working with a Vetter – and you'll be working hard!'

* * *

'Hi, I'm Gary. Pull up a chair. You're…'

'Joe Collins.'

'Right, Joe. I just have to check that you did sign the Secrecy Act paper this morning?'

'Yes, I did.'

'Right, let me show you what happens in the Books Room.' Gary was young but overweight and going bald. Joe could see why he hadn't become a Tour Guide. 'Look – here's a web site on my screen now that's come from the States. It's a publisher advertising his new books. Let's scroll down, make sure there's nothing that looks dubious.'

'Dubious?'

'Like, How to bring down the Government in six easy lessons.' He laughed. 'You'd be surprised what gets published abroad. No, looks fine. I know this publisher anyway.' He pressed a series of keys, a light went out on the big screen at the front and a new site appeared on Gary's screen. Joe saw him work on three or four before they hit a problem, a site called www.todaysgreatmen.com.

'You see, Joe, there are the names here of freedom fighters of various kinds, it could give gullible people ideas. I mean, look at the language on this one, could get people all fired up. I'm going to ban this whole thing. Want to do the dirty work? It's this key here, then that one.'

And the red light at the front clicked off.

'So that means no one in Britain will ever see that site?'

'Just us, Joe.'

'But, Gary, what's to stop people seeing the banned sites when they're on holiday abroad? Lots of people spend their evenings drinking in Net bars.'

'For a start they'd have to know what they were looking for. And what if they did find, say, some colourful lie about the Leader, well, what are they going to do with it? They'd have to be very careful who they told when they got home, they'd know they could be reported. In the same way, I'm sure that in this country there are a few illegal old PCs and Net receivers still being used, ones that aren't plugged into our control system. But their owners know they could be in trouble if they started talking about something they shouldn't have seen. Now, the next one. Tell me what you think, and I'll tell you what buttons to press if I agree.'

Ricky was tapping him on the shoulder. 'Like to finish there? Gary, would you take this lad to the front entrance? The cars are waiting there.'

'Just one thing, Gary,' said Joe as they walked along. 'How do you get to be a Tracker?'

'You're aiming high, I must say. Trackers are Vets who've done exceptional work, spotted a very subtle attack on the Leader, for example, then they've been invited to take an Advanced Skills Course. They get to know everything about how the Net works. There's no easy route, Joe. Just take one step at a time.'

Yeah, thought Joe, but you need to find out where those steps could take you.

'And the competition is fierce,' added Gary. 'Being a Vet is high enough for me. It's a comfortable life.'

I can see that, thought Joe, and promised himself, even if he got to work for the Programme, he would never become just an overweight, comfortable wage earner like Gary. The Leader was worth more than that. Being a Vet, that was step one, then came being noticed, getting on that course, becoming a Tracker. That was the dream.

But the dream had been snatched from him, torn into tiny fragments, blown away for ever. He hadn't even got to step one. Just like Joseph in fact. It wasn't just names they had in common. Had Joseph blubbered away as he went with the slave traders like Joe had done in the van? Yeah, probably. Had Joseph felt that fear that meant you couldn't stop shaking, that made you vomit? Yeah, he was sure he had. And Joseph was even worse off – he hadn't had his dad beside him as he went into captivity, hadn't had someone to pray over him when the nightmares came.

He looked up at his father, still reading the Bible, but silently now.

'Ah, Joe, you're back. I could tell you weren't listening so I stopped. It's okay.'

'Sorry. I was just thinking about Joseph's hopes and dreams. Gone.' He paused, then half smiled. Another thought had come to him, an unexpected one. 'And I guess it wasn't easy for his dad either – Jacob, wasn't that his name? He must have felt a bit responsible.'

His father's voice was very quiet. 'No, Joe, it was not easy for him. I'm sure of that.'

And Joe came across to his dad, sat beside him and put his arm round his shoulders. It wasn't necessary to say anything more.

6

There were no nightmares that night.

The next morning a new Bloomen CD arrived with the breakfast.

'Why, Dad?'

'Well, it could be there's someone up there with a guilty conscience about their job and this is their way of easing it.'

Joe remembered the look of guilt on the soldier's face in the van. 'Because I'm young, you think?'

'Or it could be an official easing of conscience, like in the US when the authorities give a last fabulous meal to prisoners on Death Row. It makes the authorities feel better, though I can imagine the prisoners have mixed feelings about it. Not that we're on Death Row, if that were the case, they'd have done it straight away. The official conscience didn't allow them to kill us, now perhaps it pushes them into giving us treats.'

But Joe preferred the idea of there being one man up there with this guilt feeling which would grow and grow until finally he could stand it no longer. The cell door would open and he'd whisper, 'It's all wrong locking up a kid like you. Quick, follow me, I'll show you the way to freedom. Your dad can come too.'

Well, perhaps not. It was a long way from giving

someone a CD to throwing in your job, even your life, for a couple of strangers. No, they might amass a CD collection that would reach the ceiling, but they wouldn't be one centimetre nearer to freedom.

But the Bloomen CD *was* fantastic and he was just about to go back to the beginning when his dad said, 'Fancy a bit more of the story?'

'Yeah. Sure.' But he wasn't sure, because the story just rubbed in the misery of his own situation. The Bloomen had created a fragile shell of sound he could hide under, like a tortoise, allowing him to pretend for a time that there was no cell and that the Lost only lived in people's imaginations. The story of Joseph cracked the shell, let the light rush in, showed him the walls of the cell all too clearly. But for his dad, it had the opposite effect. Joe could see the boost it gave him on his face, could hear it in his voice as he read.

' "Now the Ishmaelites had taken Joseph to Egypt and sold him to Potiphar, one of the king's officers, who was the captain of the palace guard. The Lord was with Joseph and made him successful. He lived in the house of his Egyptian master. Potiphar was pleased with him and made him his personal servant; so he put him in charge of his house and everything he owned." '

Joe felt a pang of jealousy. So *his* misery didn't last long, did it? All right, he couldn't lord it over his brothers, but he could lord it over the other servants instead. He'd swapped some rotten brothers and a coat for a responsible position in a rich home. Not a bad deal. As it said, 'The Lord was with him,' just another way of saying he'd done okay for himself.

' "Joseph was well-built and good-looking and after

a while his master's wife began to desire Joseph." '

Yeah, he's got it all. It's easy for him to believe in God, the way things are going.

' "But one day when he went into the house to do his work, none of the house servants was there. She caught him by his robe and said, 'Come to bed with me.' But he escaped and ran outside, leaving the robe in her hand. She called to her house servants and said, 'He came into my room and tried to rape me, but I screamed… he ran outside, leaving his robe beside me.' She kept his robe with her until Joseph's master came home. Then she told him the same story. Joseph's master was furious and had Joseph arrested and put in the prison where the king's prisoners were kept, and there he stayed." '

Joe snorted. 'So much for God then. I mean, does *he* have a nasty sense of humour or what? Just sets him up to knock him down. Twice he's done it now. I call that cruel.'

His dad looked up, frowning, and Joe wondered if he'd gone too far. He wouldn't have come out with something like that before getting in here, but now he felt less inhibited.

'I see what you mean, Joe, and I'm glad you say what's on your mind, but, well, for a start, it wasn't God who knocked him down. You can't blame God for the things people do. It was his brothers who put him in the well, not God, and it was this woman who got him arrested and put into prison. God's never nasty, Joe, never cruel. He doesn't get his kicks from knocking people down. He hates it when that happens.'

'But God *allowed* it to happen, didn't he? You've got to give me that.'

'Yes, all right. But only because he saw a purpose in it, a purpose that made it worthwhile. God had a plan, you see, he knew how it would all work out.'

'Yeah, but look, Dad, I don't want to offend you, but I've heard that so many times: God has a plan for your life, God knows what he's doing. I wonder what Joseph thought of this wonderful plan. I mean, did God check it out with him first?'

'I think, deep down, he felt okay about it. I'm sure it wasn't easy, it must have been a real shock to find himself in prison, but, well, listen to the next bit: "But the Lord was with Joseph and blessed him, so that the jailer was pleased with him. He put Joseph in charge of all the other prisoners and made him responsible for everything that was done in the prison." Think, Joe: if Joseph had turned against God, he'd be bitter and angry, and it would show: the jailer would never have given this big responsibility to someone like that. No. You can't read it any other way: Joseph must have gone on trusting God.'

Joe shrugged. 'I just don't know. Anyway it must have been horrible to think how his brothers turned against him and then how his boss' wife did the same thing.'

He was silent for a few moments, then he said quietly, 'Dad, who turned against *us*? Who got *us* into this place? The soldiers knew we were on that beach all right, knew we weren't with a group, that they could just grab us like that. Someone must have tipped them off. Someone who knows us. Who? Someone at the *Messenger*, you reckon? Dave perhaps?'

* * *

His father had been a graphic artist at the *Messenger*, one of the national daily newspapers, for almost three years. He'd always loved drawing – at school he'd got into trouble for drawing comic strips starring his teachers – and he was good at it: before he left art college, he'd had a graphic novel accepted for publication. Two more followed later. But he felt, as a single father, he needed a regular income, so he'd taken a job with a publisher helping authors with their own graphic novels, advising on layout, cover design and so on. Even Joe could see he wasn't satisfied with this. 'So why don't you do another book, Dad, instead of just helping other people?' 'I wish I had the time, Joe. But, yes, I do miss doing my own thing.'

So when the *Messenger* advertised for a graphic artist, part of whose job would be devising and drawing an original strip, he applied.

He was interviewed by Amy Ortega, the long-standing editor of the paper. ('She's quite a character, Joe, looks like everyone's favourite auntie, even wears cardigans with pretty little flowers embroidered on them. Then she opens her mouth and, well, her whisper's been known to crack contact lenses at fifty paces!')

'I like your past work, Mr Collins, but some of you people spend all day on one bit of shading and that's no use here. Look, here's a pencil and paper. I want a five frame strip with me as the main character. You've got half an hour.'

The final result, after twenty-five minutes, showed her as Queen of the Gladiators, fighting off lions whose faces looked eerily like those of the editors of rival papers. She roared with laughter, the drawings went up on the wall, and he got the job.

'Great, Dad, you'll be famous,' Joe said when his dad told him the news.

'Don't know about that, but it *is* great that the *Messenger's* produced locally, and great that they wanted a graphic artist just at this time. God must be in it.'

'I prayed for you, you know, Dad.' (Those were the days Joe said such things and meant them.)

'Well, there you are, Joe, not amazing at all then. But it's not going to be easy working there. I'll have to tread carefully – it's one of the Leader's papers.'

It had become one several years before. Amy had explained it at the interview: 'It was the only way to keep going, unless I filled the pages with pin-ups and scandal. You see, being a Leader's paper means you get press releases straight from the Leader's office. Now I couldn't afford to get the political news after my rivals – as soon as they signed up I had to. It also means we have to put up with Dave poking his nose into everything. You'll meet Dave, he'll be leaning over your shoulder too. He's the Official Representative of the Leader's Office, I think that's the proper term. Means he's a spy. He has to check everything that goes into the *Messenger*, even the readers' letters, to make sure there's nothing critical of the Leader or his policies. Anything naughty, he shouts, we cut. That's the price we pay.'

'But what's wrong with that, Dad?' said Joe when his father told him all this. 'The Leader wants what's best for the country. Anyway, doesn't affect you, does it?'

* * *

Joe met Amy for himself soon after his dad began. 'Come and meet the gang, I've told them about you. Come straight from school, that's a good time, it's quiet then, the day staff are getting ready to go home, the night staff haven't arrived. But you'd meet Auntie Amy anyway. She works day *and* night.'

She greeted him that first time with, 'Quick, give us a bit of school scandal, we need a headline for tomorrow. Something like 'Head comes to school in pyjamas! 'It's the strain of teaching Joe Collins,' he told our reporter.' Come on, otherwise the paper folds!'

So Joe got in the habit of inventing some ridiculous headline every time he visited. And every time she'd shout out, 'Stop the press! We've got a new front page!' and then a huge laugh would come gusting out of her.

Joe's dad created a number of strips in the first two years, funny, but serious too, and always beautifully drawn. The new one was to be called 'There were heroes then', comprising five large frames of detailed artwork each day about the life of a great man or woman of the past. Even the title didn't get by Dave, a small, rubbery-faced man who got very close to you when he talked. 'What does that mean, Andy? That there are no heroes now? What about the Leader then?' So the title was cut to just 'Heroes'.

Sometimes a 'life' would last a full week and would bring letters from readers who said how they'd been 'inspired' or 'uplifted' by the strip. One man wrote that it was 'a daily reminder not to be afraid of life'.

'See what a comic can do, Joe?'

'Well, it can when you're drawing it, Dad.'

Then he took a Bible character, Peter the fisherman. Amy wasn't too sure about it – a Leader's paper was not allowed to carry 'material that promotes religious belief or other outdated ways of thinking'. But Dave said, 'Well, it's not preachy – we'll see how it goes. Careful though, Andy.'

It was the fifth instalment that caused the trouble. Joe was in the office at the time, but it didn't stop Dave storming over. 'You know who that was on the phone, Andy? The Leader's office. They did not appreciate today's strip.'

'What's the problem? It's just Peter and John being arrested by the religious leaders but still refusing to stop speaking about Jesus. It's not political. It just shows what they did.'

'Yeah, but the Leader thinks you've made the main religious leader, the one being put down, looks like him.'

Andy laughed. 'Oh, that's ridiculous!'

'Well, let's ask your son,' said Dave, pushing the paper in front of Joe's face. Joe could feel Dave's hot breath oozing over the top of the sheet. 'Look, lad, that face there.'

Joe didn't want to look at the strip. He just glanced at it and shrugged. He'd never been asked to choose sides like this before.

His dad understood. 'Come off it, Dave. Let's ask Amy.'

Joe sat and waited. His father was angry when he came back and said, more to himself than to Joe, 'This is crazy. None of the faces look remotely like the Leader or any of his cronies, sorry his cabinet. It's paranoia, if you ask me!'

And that was the moment Joe began to worry about his father. It was eight months before the arrest.

But he was pleased at how everyone at the paper seemed to appreciate his dad. He heard them say things like, 'Thanks, Andy, for the new graphics for the Arts section, they really make it', or, 'Never thought of laying it out like that, great.' And Amy was delighted that circulation figures had risen, especially since the new strip appeared. 'I thought the subject might be a bit, excuse me saying it, Andy, old-fashioned, but it's really caught on.'

'People always need heroes, Amy,' he'd replied.

Joe reckoned they were a great crowd at the paper. Except for one. Not Dave, he was okay, just doing his job.

The one who spoilt it was Raymond.

Raymond started at the paper just after the Peter incident. He worked the day shift but often stayed late because, 'I got nothing special on and I like it here.' He was only three years older than Joe and had left school a year early to become an Assigned Apprentice. This was one of the Leader's schemes that gave youngsters who weren't getting on well at school a head start in a trade. The *Messenger* had been asked to take him on.

He had become a Specials Layout Assistant. In the early hours of each day, the main edition would be sent electronically to newsagents round the country who then used laser printing machines to run off as many copies as they needed for the main morning rush. Later editions, 'Specials', would come out as the day went on, most newsagents waiting for the customer to ask for the paper before printing it off. Raymond's job was to help reorganise the pages to incorporate any new stories.

Joe hated him, hated his bright little eyes, his plastered-down hair, his bony arms swinging all over the place.

'Joe, why don't you like our Raymond?' asked his dad as they left the office one evening. 'I can see it on your face every time he comes near.'

'He's pathetic. He grovels all the time, yes-sir-of-course-sir, on and on. And he grins all the time too. Drives you mad.'

'I don't think he's got much idea how to handle himself around adults. He was brought up by an elderly uncle who ill-treated him, worked him like a slave, didn't allow him much in the way of freedom. This job and the special little flat that goes with it means everything to him. He's so afraid that he's going to offend someone and lose everything that he goes over the top. Try and understand. Smile back. Reassure him.'

'All right, Dad. 'Ray, you're such an amazingly wonderful person, such speed on the keyboard, such finesse, and so humble with it, you make me ashamed of my woeful self.' Like that, you mean?'

His father laughed. 'Now you're worse than him!'

The next problem, the next that Joe knew about anyway, came three months later. The Hero was Moses.

'Andy,' murmured Dave, 'do you think you could miss out this business about Moses challenging Pharaoh? It'll remind the Leader's office of the

problem we had with Peter – it's your 'Hero' going
against recognised authority again. They won't like it. I
thought you'd appreciate *me* telling you rather than—'

'No, I don't appreciate it, Dave. We'll see Amy.
Wait here, Joe.'

It took just five minutes. He could see the result on
his dad's reddened face.

'Dad,' he said on the way home. 'Why don't you
just drop these Bible stories, stick to heroes who've
climbed mountains and healed people, stuff like that. I
mean, if the Leader doesn't like it, and he's done so
much for us and all—'

'You don't understand.'

Yeah, he thought, that's what you always say when
you don't want to give way on something.

But deep down Joe was glad his father had finished
the chat there. For the Leader was *his* hero and he did
not want to hear anything against him.

Joe looked round the cell and sighed.

'Still thinking about who betrayed us?'

'No, Dad, I didn't get that far. I was thinking about
the Leader – my... hero.'

'And what do you make of him now?'

Joe shook his head slowly. 'I just don't know.'

'For a start, was it right for him to put us in here?
Think about it.'

'Yeah.' But deep down Joe was afraid he knew the
answer already: that heroes just didn't do things like
that.

As the days went on Joe's attitude to the Joseph story
changed. He began to look forward to it, appreciating

the fact that he could make comments, all kinds of comments, and his dad didn't get offended, didn't brush what he said aside with that favourite phrase of his, 'You don't understand.'

So Joe heard how two of Joseph's fellow prisoners, servants of the king, had dreams which Joseph, with God's help, interpreted. ('He should be careful with this dreams business. It got him into right trouble first time!'). When one of the servants was released, Joseph pleaded: ' " '...mention me to the king and help me get out of this prison. I didn't do anything to deserve being put in prison.' " ' ('Surely, Dad, if God was just, Joseph wouldn't have had to plead like that. God would have helped him anyway.')

But the servant 'never gave Joseph another thought'. ('Yeah, that's encouraging for us, isn't it, Dad?') Then the king himself had dreams and no one could make out what they meant. And now, that servant remembered Joseph. He was brought up from the prison and told the king the meaning of his dreams, that the country had to prepare for a time of famine, and someone had to be appointed to organise food storage in the good years leading up to it.

Then his dad leant forward and read. ' "The king said to Joseph, 'God has shown you all this, so it is obvious that you have greater wisdom and insight than anyone else. I will put you in charge of my country.' " ' He stopped reading and looked up. 'You see, Joe, why Joseph had to be in that prison – God had a plan and now it's working out. It was a plan for the good not only of Joseph but the whole of Egypt.'

Joe grinned. 'Yeah, all right, you win. But still Joseph had to go through bad times on the way.

He didn't deserve that.'

'God knows how much we can take. I know that's easy to say, but I believe it's true.'

'So, does he know how much *we* can take? I mean, what you're saying – God knows, God cares, he's working it out, all that stuff – does it go for *us*, does it go for *now*?'

'Yes, Joe, I believe it does.'

'Well, when's his plan for *us* going to work out then? When's something going to happen to *us*? When?'

'In God's time, Joe. The right time. I hope, soon.'

7

And something did happen. But nothing they might have expected.

The routines of the day were well established now: exercises while they waited for breakfast, and again in the afternoon ('Call those press-ups, Dad? It's more like a snake wriggling along!'), and reading the Bible when the breakfast things had been taken away – though they never got far before Joe's comments and questions began.

One question Joe asked surprised his father. 'Dad, when I was young and you read the Bible to Mum and me, you always prayed aloud afterwards. Why don't you do that now?'

'I guess I didn't want to embarrass you. Or me, to be honest.'

'Oh. Well, it's okay, I won't be embarrassed. I mean you can do all the speaking and I'll just say 'Amen' at the end. All right?'

'Yes, Joe, I'd love to.'

So a new routine began, not only praying after the reading, but at the end of the day as well. Joe's dad would thank God that he saw where they were, and pray that he'd keep them patient and calm and work things out in his own time. Then he would pray for the prisoners around them, and for Christians in other parts of the world, imprisoned for their faith. As the prayer went on, Joe would think about how his nightmares had stopped when his dad prayed, and about the man who had visited the church who, despite all the suffering experienced by the Christians in his homeland, still believed in prayer, still went round asking people to pray, still believed there was someone listening. It didn't seem so easy these days just to murmur 'crazy' to himself as he had done in the past. Certainly, if there *was* a God, then it was logical to pray to him and trust him.

But for Joe that was a mighty big 'if'. For *if* there was a God, then it meant a load of people were wrong, including the Leader. He sighed, shook his head. He couldn't get his mind round it. It was too big. *Could* the Leader be wrong? Well, as his dad said, he'd put them in here and that had to be wrong. Joe noticed that the Leader was never mentioned in the prayers, but he was pretty sure his dad prayed for him afterwards, maybe that he would lose his position as Leader, definitely that he'd become a Christian. Perhaps his dad was a bit worried how Joe would take his 'hero' being prayed for like that.

No, he just didn't know what he thought any more. About anything. But he liked to hear his dad praying. Partly because it helped him remember when he was young, it helped him visualise his mum, how she would sit so still during the prayers, except for sometimes biting her lip. He'd loved her quietness, missed that more than anything. Funny that. He also liked the prayer time because it made him peaceful inside. Although he didn't listen to every word his dad said, he was always a bit sad when it came time to say 'Amen'.

Then it happened. The unexpected.

Joe got toothache.

It was so painful that, even though it was the middle of the night, he had to wake his dad up. They prayed, but the pain didn't ease. Finally the hatch bell rang and they could use the mike.

'My son has toothache, really bad. He needs treatment, a dentist. And do you have any pills to relieve the pain in the meantime?'

The pills came within minutes. Three hours later the door slid open. Two guards – ones they'd not seen before – entered. Without a word, they blindfolded Joe and led him away.

8

'Remember everything – sounds, smells, how long it takes to get from one place to another, every word they say. There could be some clue as to how we get out of here. I'll be praying.'

Those were his dad's last words before the door slid open. Now Joe heard it shut behind him, but the effect of the pills had worn off and it was hard to focus on anything except the pain – it seemed to be tearing his jaw off.

Come on! He told himself. Think! Now we're in the lift, yes, they're turning me round, we're going up.

Then it struck: his dad had assumed they would get in some mobile dentist, but what if they were taking him outside? Surely that was more likely. Surely. In which case, come on! You've got to be ready! Forget the pain, you mustn't miss the chance when it comes! He tried to think it through. There'll be the guards around, but they'd have to take the blindfold off, it'd look suspicious when they got him out of the van, then, yes! There was *bound* to be someone around, in the street, or some other patient maybe – someone he could get a message to, even if it was just a couple of words, a message that could blow this 'Lost' business sky-high. He'd just need a couple of seconds.

He thought of the day they'd come in here. He knew, if they were taking him outside, they'd turn left out of the lift.

The lift stopped, the door hummed open. He felt the pressure on his arms increase. They stepped forward. Left now! Left!

They turned him right. Away from the outside world. That was that. There would be no chance, no message. He felt sick with frustration.

Then the pain slammed in again. It seemed even worse now.

He gulped in air to steady himself. It was stale and dry, as if it had been breathed in and out too many times, and there was some chemical polluting it. But the smell reminded him of his dad's words: remember – smells, sounds, everything. Come on, Joe! he told himself. Don't give in!

A voice… they were going towards it. 'Oh. Right. Wasn't expecting a child. Let's have him on here then.'

He felt himself held under the arms, then his legs being lifted. He was put on a hard couch. Was it some sort of dentist's chair?

'Where's the problem?'

So they had got someone in. But there could still be a clue, that's what Dad reckoned. So think! Listen!

'I said, where's the problem? I'm talking to you!'

Joe flinched. The voice was right by his ear. He hadn't realised it was for him. He put a finger in his mouth and pointed to where the pain was worst.

'What? That one?' Joe felt something tap against the tooth. He shook his head. 'That one?' Joe jerked away, couldn't stop himself shuddering. 'Right. Well, we know where it is now.'

Joe felt hands on his shoulders – there was someone behind him.

'Wider.'

A finger brushed his cheek. He shrank back into the seat, felt a touch of cold on his gum. Anaesthetic. Something hard knocked against his top lip as it was put in his mouth and he heard a drill start up, one of the old-fashioned ones, noisy. He felt the muffled pressure of the drilling, nothing else.

'Rinse.' It was over. The hands moved from his shoulders, a beaker was pushed against his fingers. After some fumbling he got hold of it, gargled, spat, not caring whether there was anything held to catch it. There must have been, no one shouted.

Silence, apart from a soft clicking sound behind him.

He could think now. The dentist was an older man, he wouldn't mind betting, and he had a raspy voice, probably from smoking too much – Joe could smell the sourness on his breath. Outside he'd have had a mask on, he wasn't bothering in here. As for the hands on his shoulders, was it a woman? He could smell some kind of scent.

'Thanks. I might want more than that.' The dentist again, the voice very close, but the words addressed to the someone who'd been making the clicking sound – the nurse making the filling mixture?

'What's for pudding today?' He'd turned his head, must be talking to the guards now. 'Anything good?'

'Kind of chocolate tart. It's all right.'

'Go on then. Go down and get me some if it's ready. I need some kind of reward for coming here in this weather. Want some? Right, just me then. And make the coffee hot this time, okay?' All said in a jokey way.

Joe could hear one of the guards moving away, softly whistling as he went, then a sort of quick patting noise. Stairs? Yes, must be stairs – the dentist had said: go down, and there'd been no sound of a lift closing.

'Come on, open up.' Something small entered his mouth, began pressing down on the tooth. He tried to get his breathing in time with the dentist's so he wouldn't have to take in his sour breath. He hoped he was wearing gloves, as one of his fingers was leaning on Joe's wet bottom lip. He felt he was going to vomit. Yeah, great, who cares anyway? But, then again, what if they took him back to the cell stinking of it? Not great. He swallowed hard.

The guard returned. 'On here, okay?' The sound of metal on metal – tray on table?

'Yeah, thanks. Took you long enough. Thought you'd taken to your bed.'

'No chance with those food mixers going. Worse noise than your drill.'

The filling pusher or whatever it was called was taken from his mouth, his lip sticking to the dentist's finger for a second.

'Right, that's that. Stay there.'

Joe understood the dentist meant him. Clicking sounds now, spoon on cup, cup on tray. No complaints about cold coffee. Someone was happy then. Very slowly, Joe began to lift his left hand, the one furthest away from the noises, towards the blindfold. Immediately a hand clasped his wrist, pushing it back. Well, it was worth a try.

'Yeah, not bad. Prefer the apple strudel you had last time.' The dentist was moving about while he was speaking. 'We'd better dash. Couldn't cancel the twelve o'clock one.'

'Right. They'll be needing help with the lunches soon anyway.' It was the guard who'd gone for the coffee.

Joe felt his body being swivelled into a sitting position.

'Stand up.' The other guard this time.

'Cheers then.' The dentist.

'Bye.' Yes, a female, young sounding. The first female voice he'd heard since it had happened. He suddenly thought of Anna, thought of the rock concert they'd been planning to go to together.

And he couldn't stop it: he opened his mouth, felt his tongue still numb from the anaesthetic, but went for it anyway, shouted it out, 'Help!' It came out distorted but surely they could catch the desperation in his voice. Had the dentist heard? Had *she* heard? Did she realise he was a prisoner in here? He tried again. 'Help! Help!'

Now both his arms were being gripped. They were dragging him back to the lift.

'No! No! I won't go back! I want to go home!' But the words were running into each other, a blurred shriek. He had to do more – they'd be gone in a moment and they had to take him with them, they had to. So he shook himself, this way, that way, tried to kick, this way, that way, all the time yelling out, 'I won't go back! I won't go back!'

Then he felt himself being spun round and frog-marched, fast. 'No! No!' His feet were dragging, his heels making a screeching noise on the floor. He tried to put them flat to pull himself upright, but couldn't do it.

He heard the door at the end of the room slide open – the door to the outside. His last chance. He screamed as loud as he could, not bothering to make a word now.

Before the sound had died away, he was turned again, into the lift. He just had time to hear the dentist say, 'Don't worry, they'll look after him.' Then the lift door clicked shut.

And the fight went out of him. He slumped back against the doors, letting the guards support him.

'Steady, lad.' It was the coffee guard. 'Stand up now.'

They pulled him up, turned him round. The lift stopped.

He sucked in air, tried to control his breathing. The door opened, but they didn't move until he said, 'Yeah, I'm okay now.' It hurt him to speak but the words were clearer already. The pressure on his arms was lighter now.

Twelve paces. Yes. He'd got himself together all right. Any second, that sliding noise. There.

'Step.'

Yes, he knew.

Then he felt hands tearing off the blindfold, more familiar hands round his shoulders.

'All right, Joe? How's it feeling, did they do it all right?'

Joe nodded.

The guards were stepping out of the cell now. Then one of them turned, looked directly at his father and said in a slightly shaky voice, 'It's lunch soon.' Joe recognised the voice of the coffee guard, a man of about his dad's age, pale and tall with wispy fair hair.

'Right, let's go,' said the other guard, a shorter,

darker man, pressing a button on his belt. The pale one pressed a similar button. He was still gazing at his dad when the door slid shut.

'That's him, isn't it?' said Joe. 'The fair-haired one, I mean. He's the one who sends us things.'

'How do you know that?'

'I don't really know it, I just… I mean, why'd he bother saying that about lunch? Why'd he stare at you like that? It's as if he wanted to make contact and that's all he could think of to say.'

'You might be right. But what's important now is what you learnt.'

Joe sighed and moved his jaw around, pleased his voice was steady, that his dad couldn't tell the state he'd been in just a few moments before. But what exactly had he learnt? Nothing of any use, surely. 'Well, I learnt there's chocolate tart for lunch and it's not as good as apple strudel.' Joe shrugged. 'Honestly, Dad, I don't know what you expected me to find out. They never took the blindfold off, you know.'

'Just go through the whole thing.'

So Joe did, omitting only what had happened at the end. No need to mention that. Ever. When he'd finished, his dad asked, 'And those were the exact words the dentist said when he asked for the pudding?'

'Yeah, but so what?'

'Because our freedom, Joe, may depend on just one of his words. But don't ask me yet. I'll tell you the whole thing when I've thought it through.'

Hearing that should have been the most exciting moment for Joe since this had all started. But instead it made him feel sick. Was his dad losing it? He just couldn't believe any plan could depend on one word from a dentist. What word? Chocolate? Go? And?! It was ridiculous. Joe would normally have badgered his father to tell him his plan, told him to stop treating him like a child, but he didn't now. Because his father wouldn't have anything to say. There was no one word, no 'whole thing' to think through. It was a fantasy, like his own idea that the dentist and the nurse would take him with them if he made enough noise. Sad old dad, he thought. Bad as me.

'And how's the tooth?'

'Sorry? Oh, yeah, It was an old-fashioned drill and a smelly old dentist. But, yeah, okay. I'm ready to eat. Come on, lift.'

But when the bell rang and they opened the hatch it wasn't just the food containers they saw. For lodged between the containers was a small book. Joe's dad picked it up. It was an old, obviously much-read copy of John Bunyan's *Pilgrim's Progress*.

'Joe,' he said quietly. 'I think you're right. I think we've got a friend up there.'

'It's a great classic, but it's been out of print for years. This is one of those pocket editions that were popular when I was young. Yes, here's the date it was printed, 2006. Look, the corner's missing on the title page. I bet our guard had his name in it, but he tore it out in case the authorities got hold of it and didn't like his taste.' He was holding the book reverently, turning the pages slowly as if they would crumble if he went too fast.

'But why this book, Dad? We didn't ask for it.'

'He must know we asked for a Bible, so he'd guess at least one of us is a Christian. And this is one of the greatest Christian books ever written.'

'So he's a Christian too?'

'Maybe. But I think there's another reason why it's this book. It was written in prison, where Bunyan had been put for being too enthusiastic about Jesus. He'd wanted to make the gospel available to everyone, not just the people who went to church. I'd have loved to have drawn his story for the strip, but I think Dave would have had a fainting fit. He was a rebel all right, of the best kind. It'll be something good to read together.' He glanced up at Joe. 'If you want to.'

It didn't sound a very cheerful book, but he just said, 'Yeah, all right. After we've finished with Joseph though.'

They had already read how famine came to Canaan, Joseph's homeland, at the same time as Egypt. But Canaan, unlike Egypt, had no storehouses full of grain, so Jacob decided to send his remaining sons over the border to beg for anything the Egyptians could spare.

The brothers had been ushered into the presence of the man in charge of food storage, who recognised them but kept his own identity hidden. They bowed down before him...

'Like in his first dream, you remember, Joe, when their sheaves bowed down to his.'

'Surely they'd have recognised their own brother. Come on!'

'But this is a good few years later. They didn't expect to see him, and he'd be in Egyptian costume. He'd look very different from when they saw him last.'

Then he'd read about how the brothers were different now too, on the inside. They'd spent those last years seeing the grief of losing his favourite son on their father's face, and regretting what they'd done. But they couldn't bring Joseph back, and they didn't have the courage to admit they had lied (they'd made out to Jacob a wild animal had killed him). As they grew older and wiser, they became more and more ashamed.

So when Joseph tested them by framing Jacob's new favourite, Benjamin, for stealing from the palace, they pleaded with Joseph, one of them even offering to take Benjamin's punishment.

Now Joe's dad read on, about how Joseph, seeing they were changed men, revealed who he was and told them he forgave them for the past and how God had worked it all out for good.

'Forgave them? Dad, that's not fair. Even though it worked out right, the brothers still deserved to be punished. I mean, think what they put Joseph through. They didn't know he'd land on his feet like that.'

'But he did forgive them, Joe. I can't change the ending. He forgave them and he proved it by inviting them to live near him in Egypt. You see, it wasn't just words.'

'Well, I think he was daft. Great story though.' Joe had to admit that.

That night Joe found it difficult to sleep. He was thinking of what his dad had talked about that morning: freedom. But the flicker of hope he felt was not based on the rest of what his dad had said, this great plan he had to think through, but based on what a pale-faced guard had said: 'It's lunch soon.'

Could it have been a coded message that something else might be 'soon' too?

9

Despite the problem getting to sleep, Joe woke early
the next morning. He lay gazing up at the pale blue
ceiling: like a plastic sky, he thought, with the neon
strip a stretched out sun. He smiled to himself, half-
closed his eyes to increase the illusion, then began
rocking himself gently from side to side. Yes, he could
hear the slap of the waves now, could feel the solidness
of the kayak under him – wonderful. He raised his
arms, began sweeping the paddle through the water,
gently at first, then faster and faster. He was skipping
over the waves now, using the current, not fighting it,
moving as if the kayak and paddle were parts of his
body, sensing he could do anything, go anywhere,
feeling he could soar into the sky any second. True
freedom – freedom to fly!

He became aware of his dad's light snoring and let
his hands drop onto the blanket.

His dad? Funny, he didn't feel much like a dad these
days. More like an older brother. Having his hair cut
really short had helped, it had taken years off him. But
it wasn't mainly how he looked. It was more about the
relationship. Down here he didn't need to ask his dad's
permission to do something, to go somewhere, like he
used to. So he wasn't being reminded all the time that

he wasn't the one in charge. They seemed more equal now, more like each other, even taking on each other's roles. His dad was more ready to explain himself, more ready to say sorry – usually Joe's part. Joe himself was more willing, if there was a disagreement, to listen calmly and not storm off in a huff. There were no doors to slam here of course and no mates to phone for reassurance, but even so, he wanted to talk things over with his dad now, wanted to know where he was coming from. They'd both stopped pretending to know it all, that was it. The pressures to be the wise, responsible parent and the slightly rebellious teenager weren't there any more.

Yeah, great lessons. Joe bit his lip. Shame they couldn't have been learnt above ground.

And the thought slammed back. Who'd got them into this? Who'd betrayed them? Who?

He'd stopped himself thinking much about this. He didn't want to know, afraid that he'd hate the person so much that the hate would soil everything he said and did. It was better that the hate was unfocussed: *They* had put them in here. *They* were to blame. He could think about *Them* without his stomach turning over. Sure, he thought about the Vulture and the soldiers at times, even thought about the policeman who had pushed over his mother, but he couldn't hate them for very long, he just didn't know them well enough.

But the betrayer was different. He had to be someone they knew. And he wasn't just doing a job like the soldiers. He'd made a choice to contact the authorities and say, 'You can get them now. They're with their kayak. It's a lonely bit of coast. I'll tell you exactly where.' It had to be someone who knew the spot, who'd been there.

Someone in Dad's church? Could be, several of them had boats or wave skimmers and had gone with them on odd occasions. No, no good, it couldn't be any of them: they didn't know they were going that day.

So it had to be someone on the day shift at the paper, someone who'd seen them go and knew exactly where they were going. Big help. They all knew those cliffs, that stretch of beach, that track through the trees. They'd have known since the beginning of the summer, since Amy's barbecue...

'Sorry, one and all, can't use my back garden for the staff do this year. Having a conservatory built. Any ideas?' Amy looked round the newsroom.

His dad had said, 'Well, it's a bit of a drive, but Joe and I take the kayak to a great spot.'

Someone asked him how it was for kids – families of staff came on the outing too.

'Yes, great. The swimming's safe, and there are steps down the cliffs, they aren't sheer anyway.'

And parking?

'Right on the grass at the top, and there are loos in the park about a mile away, we can organise runs in the cars, no problem.'

'All agreed then?' said Amy. 'Shall we go with that?'

It was to be Amy's treat as always, her way of saying thanks to her loyal staff for keeping the paper going. She brought all the food and cooked it pretty much single-handedly. Not just burgers and sausages ('for uneducated stomachs'), but steaks stuffed with oysters, huge prawns and ribs of pork with what she called 'Stop Press Sauce'. But Joe was still looking forward to the burgers most: they were The Best.

He had been to two of these staff barbecues before, so he knew how differently some of the adults behaved compared with when they were at work: who would have believed Dave would be the games organiser for a start? But Joe wasn't expecting Raymond, whom he'd never seen out of the newsroom, to act like he did.

As soon as they arrived, he charged down the steps to the beach with most of the younger children streaming behind him. Then he was a seagull, arms stretched out, swooping over the sands, making cawing noises punctuated with high pitched whoops. Some of the children copied him, others just stood and gazed at him.

There were spectators at the top of the cliff too.

'He's mad,' said Joe. 'I mean, look at him. He's older than me.'

'But you see what he's doing,' said Amy. 'He's learning to play. When he was with his uncle, he had to be the little adult, the servant of the house. He's never been allowed to be a child, he's got some catching up to do. So he's not mad, Joe, and he's not dim. Just let him enjoy himself for once, all right?'

Joe turned away. The sight of Raymond 'playing' made him feel a bit sick.

His dad had brought along their Neptuna Medallion two-man kayak and offered a free trip along the coast to anyone who wanted it – 'Just promise to be sick over the side, not over me.' Joe felt a slight sting of jealousy when the first taker sat in his place in the boat, and he wished he'd argued a bit more for leaving it at home. But the feeling had almost gone – when Raymond stepped up for his turn. Bounced up more like it, thought Joe: with his spindly legs and flapping arms he's more like a demented ostrich than a human being.

His dad was holding the boat steady. 'Come on, Ray, best take your shoes off. Now, clamber in, try to keep your weight over the centre of the boat. No, no, that leg first... slide the leg in... steady... you're in. Joe, will you hold it while I get in?'

Joe splashed out to the boat, saw Ray glance up at him and, seeing his expression, look down again quickly.

Then they were away. Joe gazed after them. Ray was swinging his paddle like he was smacking the air, hardly making contact with the water at all. Pathetic.

But, all in all, it was a good day.

'Joe, I want to ask you something,' said his dad when they got home. 'Did you see our Ray in the kayak? I tell you, I've never seen anyone so excited, and we only went along the coast a bit. He was so appreciative. It would do him a world of good, Joe, if we took him with us sometimes. I could teach—'

'Has 'our Ray' got a kayak then? No. Well then.'

'Joe, listen, there's that old one of mine in the garage, we could take that as well. I'd take him out for a bit of tuition while you—'

'While I paddle about in that crummy—'

'Joe, don't keep interrupting me.'

'You just interrupted me. I don't see why we have to do this. We don't owe him anything.'

'Just think about it. We go down every week. I was just thinking every second or third week.'

Joe started towards his room, his shoulders lowered. 'Sounds like you've planned it all out anyway.'

'No, Joe, I—' The door slammed.

Over breakfast the next morning, Joe murmured, 'Okay then. Every third week. If he's that keen.'

'Great. Though I don't know what the Eskimo rolls are going to do for his hair-style.' He smiled but Joe wouldn't look up.

The next time Joe came to the newsroom, Raymond waved at him. 'Can I have a word in private, like? In the passage?'

'If you want.'

'Joe, I just want to say thank you, like, for agreeing to me going out in the kayak sometimes. I know… I know you don't like me, and that's okay, I'd think the same if I knew me.' He gave a nervous little laugh. 'And it would have been dead simple for you to have said no to your dad and he would have gone along with you, I know that, but, well, it was big of you, and well, thanks.'

'Oh.' Joe shrugged, looking anywhere but at Ray. ''s all right.'

He stayed in the passage thinking after Ray had gone. What had he said? 'Your dad… would have gone along with you…' Yeah, it was true. If he'd said no to Ray, Dad wouldn't have pushed it, wouldn't have even mentioned it again, because he wouldn't want Joe to think he was putting him anywhere but first. But Ray had probably never had anyone who'd put him first – or second or anywhere. That pig of an uncle wouldn't have thought of what Ray wanted. Joe felt a bit bad about not saying yes to his dad straight away.

'My paddles are going to be a bit short for him, Dad.'

'He'll be okay. It's easier for beginners if they have shorter paddles.'

'As long as he can find the water with them this time round. No, Dad, I won't make fun of him. That's a promise.'

It was hard to keep it though. Ray sat in the front of the two-man kayak this time. Joe paddled about in the shallows waiting for the disaster to happen.

'Ray, watch the blade as it goes into the water. Twist it, look at Joe doing it, can you get that angle? Yes, better, but now you're scraping the side. Put it further out... that's right. Don't hunch yourself up – sit up straight, lad.'

After an hour, Joe and his dad left Ray on the beach guarding the old kayak ('Don't get any ideas, Ray, you're not ready yet') while they put the Medallion to the test. They built up speed till all Joe could see of his arms and paddle was a blur. They were really racing, it was incredible – like freewheeling down a steep hill on a bike, no, more like skiing down Everest! Joe knew it was his dad's way of rewarding him. Joe was still first.

They saw it when they got back to the beach. Ray had collected stones and laid them out on a strip of sand to read, 'GREAT'. He stood there, pointing at the word and grinning.

After the second time, Joe said, 'I mean, Dad, summer's short. Every third week's not much. I don't mind if he comes every week. What do you think?'

And week by week, Ray relaxed more, took things more steadily and really got the hang of it.

Then came the day of the arrest.

'You ready, Ray? Dad's just tidying up. Then we'll be off.'

Ray looked up from his screen. 'Mmm? Oh yeah… be right with you.'

Joe could see he wasn't well. There were beads of sweat glistening on his forehead and his eyes didn't seem able to focus on Joe's face. 'You okay?'

'Oh… yeah. See you in the car park.'

Joe and his dad were in the car when he sidled over. He got in the back seat but left the door open. 'I… I can't come,' he murmured. 'I'm not well, you see. You're going, are you? I mean, I don't know what the weather's—'

'The weather's fine, just right. So of course we're going. Come on, lad, it'll do you good.'

Joe had a vision of Ray being sick into his hair as they drove along and almost said, 'Don't force him, Dad.'

'No. I must go home.' Ray pushed himself out of the car.

'Can we give you a lift then?'

He didn't reply, just stood by the car. Then he lifted his hands to the kayaks on the roof, ran his fingers along the edge of the Medallion and, without saying a word, hurried off.

'Next time then,' Joe shouted after him.

But Ray didn't turn round. And there was no next time. In a little over two hours they would be meeting the Vulture.

Now his dad was awake, sitting on the edge of the bed, scratching his head. Joe could hear the hum of the lift beginning its deliveries.

'It was Ray, wasn't it? Wasn't it, Dad?'

His father looked up at him for a moment, then said, 'Yes, I think it was.'

'I mean, it had to be. He was the only one who knew we'd be alone. But why, Dad? I mean, we went out of our way to be friends with him.'

'I don't think that had anything to do with it, Joe. I imagine the powers-that-be looked at those last strips and thought: this Andrew Collins has to go. But how? We can't be seen arresting him. We need someone to tell us when there's no one around. Now, who'll do that little job for us? Ah, perfect, our Raymond. "Be a good boy, Raymond. You do owe us, you know. We got you a flat, a job. Oh, we've been so good to you, Raymond. Now show a bit of appreciation. Your colleague, Collins, we need to… talk to him. Just tell us when he's going to be alone. That's all. If you don't, the Leader may think such an ungrateful person doesn't deserve that flat, that job…" Poor Ray.'

'Poor Ray? Rubbish, Dad, he made a choice. He's guilty. He's taken away our freedom, our… lives. And for what?'

'For what he values most, Joe: independence. And I think you're wrong. I don't think he knew what was going to happen. He didn't know about this underground prison, that's for sure. He probably thought they'd just threaten me, maybe get a bit physical, but not this.'

'But he knew I'd be there at the beach.'

'The beach was all he could come up with. Perhaps he was hoping I'd go by myself one day. But I reckon they were badgering him. So he went for it, hoping they'd just run you home and tell you Daddy would be home later.'

'You're full of excuses for him.'

'I'm not excusing him at all, Joe. What he did was wrong. I'm just giving you the reason. Sometimes that can help us forgive.'

'Forgive?' Joe shouted the word. 'I'll never forgive him. I can't and I won't. I'm not like that other Joseph. I want him to suffer.'

'Don't you think he's suffering now? Remember how he looked that day, grey and sweaty? Remember how he mentioned the weather, half-hoping we wouldn't go to the beach? Even then the guilt was getting to him. Think how he felt when I didn't turn up the next day, when the news came through we'd had an accident in the kayak, presumed drowned – I imagine that's the story they put round. Then he'd have understood what he'd got into. Amy, bless her, would have run the story big time and Ray would have had to work with it for the later editions, knowing it was all lies, believing he'd become an accessory to murder.'

'Good. I hope it tears him apart.'

His father sighed. Then the bell rang and he went to open the hatch.

They washed and ate. Not that Joe was aware of any of it. He was seething, his mind full of the betrayal. If it had been Dave, he could have understood it more, he and his dad were workmates, that was all. But his dad had gone out of his way to help Ray, to show him people cared, only to have it all thrown back in his face. How could his dad sit there and talk of forgiveness? It made him sick.

Finally, he became aware of his father looking across at him. So he mumbled, 'You want to start on this book the guard sent, do you?'

'Joe, I can see what's on your mind, so, no, I'd like to read you something else instead, something from the life of Jesus. It might be helpful.'

'Helpful? It'll only be helpful if it tells me how I can get back at Ray.'

'Oh, that would satisfy you, would it?'

'Yeah, it would.'

'No, it wouldn't, Joe. It wouldn't help at all.'

Joe shrugged. 'Well, I can't put any plan of revenge into operation anyway, can I?' He managed a weak smile. 'Go on then. Life of Jesus.'

'It's the night before he was to die. He's at the Passover meal with his disciples.'

'Is that the Last Supper?'

'That's right. They were sitting down to eat. ' "During the meal Jesus said, 'I tell you, one of you will betray me.' The disciples were very upset and began to ask him, one after the other, 'Surely, Lord, you don't mean me?' Jesus answered, 'One who dips his bread in the dish with me will betray me. The Son of Man will die as the Scriptures say he will, but how terrible for that man who betrays the Son of Man...' Judas, the traitor, spoke up. 'Surely, Teacher, you don't mean me?' he asked. Jesus answered, 'So you say.' " '

He looked across at Joe. 'You see, Jesus was getting on the religious leaders' nerves. They were intensely jealous, they wanted him out of the way. But the crowd loved him, so the leaders had to think, 'How can we get to him without causing a riot?' The answer came when Judas sidled up to them and said, 'What will you give me if I betray Jesus to you?' So they agreed on thirty silver coins and Judas waited for the time when

Jesus would be vulnerable.'

'I see. Judas equals Ray.'

'A little bit, yes. Anyway, that time has now come. After that Last Supper, Jesus would be going out with his disciples onto the Mount of Olives – a dark, lonely spot. That's it, Judas must have thought, it's ideal. I'll find an excuse to leave the meal and get things moving. Now, Jesus knew exactly what was going on in his mind, but he goes on showing Judas love, sharing bread with him, warning him of the terrible consequences if he goes ahead with the betrayal. And when Judas leads a crowd of heavies out to grab Jesus, what does Jesus do? He calls Judas 'friend'. The traitor had given the crowd a signal: "The man I kiss is the one you want. Arrest him!" Judas went straight to Jesus and said, "Peace be with you, Teacher," and kissed him. Jesus answered, "Be quick about it, friend!" Then they came up, arrested Jesus and held him tight. And, you know, Joe, Jesus wasn't being sarcastic saying 'friend'. He could have taken revenge in a thousand ways, but he didn't. He was always ready to forgive, and he went on like that – with the soldiers who nailed him to the cross, with Peter who let him down by denying he knew him. And he's like it today, Joe. Ready to forgive anyone who's turned his back on him in the past, ready and waiting to welcome them back. And we should have the same attitude. As far as Ray is concerned...'

But Joe wasn't listening any more. He'd got hooked on the words, 'anyone who's turned his back on him in the past'. Turned his back on him...

And suddenly Joe remembered, so clearly that it was frightening, and it had nothing to do with

Raymond. It was the last year in School 2. His classroom. He was there again by Mr Webb's desk, heard him say again, 'May I make a suggestion? Decide where your loyalties lie... do you get my meaning?' And Joe had burbled, 'I can't suddenly stop going to church... But I am committed to the Leader, I am.' So quick, so easy. God pushed away with one hand. No problem.

So: Joseph's brothers. Judas. Ray. And Joe. Traitors, all of them. They'd all made a choice. Get rid of Joseph. Sell Jesus. Put independence above friendship. Put the Leader and what he offered above God.

He glanced up at his father, quiet now, watching him. 'Did you know about Mr Webb, Dad?' It was barely a whisper.

'Was he the one who made you the deal, Joe?' His voice was very gentle. 'I knew something had happened, what with you saying you couldn't go to church so often. It came so suddenly. Then, later, that invitation to the Net Centre. I guessed there might be some connection. But, Joe, you were younger then, I'm not sure you knew what you were doing, not sure you knew what you were turning your back on.'

'I still made a choice, Dad.'

'Then understand, Joe, that you can remake that choice. Anytime. That's why Jesus died – to keep the door open. I think you understand more about both sides now. It's up to you.'

Joe looked up. He knew what his dad wanted, what he longed for. But he couldn't do it. It was too big a jump. There was so much he wasn't sure of.

'Joe – when you're ready, okay?'

Joe nodded. Not yet then. Not yet.

'Shall I just pray as normal then?'

Joe nodded again. But he felt every word of the prayer leaning on him, pinning him down, while the Big Question hovered in the air around him: do you want this God, this Jesus, for yourself?

But what difference could this God make to his life? Down here? And even if he could make a difference, did he want it? Then other questions joined in: is he there at all? Is he just a bunch of nice, soothing words and ideas? Is all this just some fantasy? He couldn't get his thoughts clear at all.

Then came the Amen and he breathed again. For once, the prayer hadn't calmed him down. Just the opposite. For he knew he'd never be able to make flippant remarks or sarcastic jokes about these things again, never be able to smile as he pointed out what he saw as a contradiction in the Bible or something wrong in God's personality. This was serious now.

He needed time to think. He didn't want his father to go on talking about this choice any more. Not now. Change the subject then. He said the first thing that came into his mind.

'Have you thought through your plan of escape, Dad? Ready to tell me yet?'

His father's answer sent a shiver through his whole body. It wasn't what he expected at all.

'Funny you should mention that, Joe. Yes, I have thought it through. We can begin tonight.'

10

Joe could see this wasn't a joke. His dad looked dead serious.

But it was ridiculous. How could they 'begin tonight'? How could they 'begin' anything, any time? They were surrounded – four walls, a ceiling, a floor. 'I have thought it through,' he'd said. But what was there to think through?

'Dad—'

'I'm going exploring, Joe. I was about to tell you when—'

'Exploring?' What was going on? Which corner of the cell was he going to explore?

His dad smiled. 'Now you're thinking I've gone completely crazy. Well, we'll see. I don't know myself how far I'll get.'

'Dad, how are you going to get *anywhere*? This is a prison cell.'

'A prison cell with transport though.' And he pointed at the lift.

'Dad, you can't go up in that! What are going to do, disguise yourself as a bucket? I mean—'

'I'm not planning on going in it, Joe. I'm planning on going on top of it, getting on board as it comes up on its last journey from the cell below. Listen. You remember when you were on the top floor the dentist told the guard to go *down* – that was the key word – to the kitchen to get the tart. I'm assuming that's just one floor down. So I reckon if I'm standing on top of the lift when it's stationary at the kitchen, I should be able to reach up to the hatch that leads to that top floor.'

Joe gazed at him. 'How do you know there'll be a hatch? You had a blindfold on same as me when they walked us through.'

'I don't *know* anything, Joe. I'm making guesses. But I bet that top floor's where they do the laundry. Do you remember that dry chemical smell?' Yes, Joe had smelt it when he'd gone up to the dentist too. 'Well then, it's logical for the lift to go all the way up. They aren't going to carry laundry up and down stairs.'

'But, Dad, even if there's a hatch, and even if you can get through somehow – so what? The guards could be right on the other side of it.'

'No, not if I wait on the lift until the guards are asleep. Don't you remember, the dentist jokingly wondered if the guard had gone to bed, he'd taken so long getting his snack. So they must sleep on the same floor as the kitchen, not on the laundry floor. And I bet there's no night guard anyway. Why should there be?'

'Yeah, so you've escaped to the laundry. Great. There are still two electronically controlled doors to get through.'

'There must be another way. Just think: why do they blindfold you when you're on that floor? Both times they've done it. Because, Joe, there's some weakness in the system, something they don't want you to see. I reckon it's to do with that chimney we saw when we came, do you remember? That big green pipe sticking out about two metres from the ground. I bet there's a way into that chimney.'

'You're guessing, Dad, guessing all the way.'

'If I'm wrong, then I'll find out.'

Then it sank in and Joe's heart started hammering away. *I'm* going exploring, he'd said. *I'll* find out, he'd said. Always *I*, never *we*.

'What... what about me? You're not... leaving me?'

His father grinned. 'Ah, so you do think it's a possibility I'll make it out then! No, Joe, I'm not leaving you, I wouldn't do that.'

'Then I'm coming too?'

'No, there's too much unknown in it, I can't risk it. For a start...' He stopped. Joe could see he was wondering whether to say it. 'For a start, I don't *know* if the lift stays at the kitchen floor overnight. I *think* it does – there's no logical reason for it to go up to the laundry floor. We get fresh clothes on Sunday and Wednesday mornings, like all the cells served by this lift – the guard told us that on the first day. Today's Thursday, so they won't be loading any clothes onto the lift tonight. Or tomorrow, Joe.'

He understood now. 'That's when we—'

'When we both go. If I can find that weakness. I'll stay up there tonight and come down with the breakfast for the cell below.'

'But the hatch here will be closed. How will you get off? And how will you get on to start with?'

'I went into that while you were a million miles away with the Shams. The prong on my belt buckle is exactly the same size as the catch on the hatch door. So we don't close the hatch, we just push the prong into the lock on the wall and the lift mechanism should start. Up above, they'll never know it's open.' He smiled. 'Joe, I can't guarantee it'll lead to anything. But as I've prayed, I've felt God saying, 'Go for it!''

Joe couldn't speak. He was aware of a dreadful coldness seeping into him. He knew he should be feeling excited. But he wasn't. It was all 'if' this, and 'I think' that. It was all a risk. Too much of a risk. There were a thousand things that could go wrong. For a start, what if the lift didn't stop at the kitchen floor? What if it went all the way up? His dad, on top of the lift, would be…

He gazed around the cell, biting his lip. Wouldn't it be better to stay down here? It wasn't too bad, they had food and they had each other. And it was safe. Nothing could go wrong, nothing bad could happen. But if Dad went on that lift…

'Couldn't we – couldn't we wait and see if that guard gets us out? The one who sent the book. He could be working on some plan now. He could be down tonight.' He was aware of speaking too fast, his voice shaking a bit.

'Joe, do you really believe that? I don't.'

'But, Dad, I can't leave.' He was beginning to panic now. 'I just can't. I-I've got my CDs here!'

His dad laughed out loud. Hearing it, the bubble of fear that had been welling up in Joe burst, and he laughed too, at the sheer daftness of what he'd said. Neither of them could stop. When the giggling began to subside, his dad just pointed to the CDs on the bed and they were off again.

'Surely, Dad, if it was possible to escape, someone would have done it by now.'

'I doubt that they've even tried. They've seen how powerful the Leader is and they reckon he'd have made escape impossible and so they give up. But is that how it is? I reckon this place was put up – well, put down really – in a hurry, probably it was the first of its kind, and there could easily be some weak spot. I believe God's going to help us find it. In this book,' and he held up the battered copy of *Pilgrim's Progress*, 'two of the characters, called Christian and Hopeful, are put in a kind of prison called Doubting Castle. They feel totally crushed, suicidal. Then Christian remembers he has a key on him called Promise, God's promise, of his power, his help, his presence always—'

'Dad, you're beginning to preach.'

'Well, you get the idea. They believe in this key so they use it and it gets them out. I think the other prisoners here are trapped not just by the walls but by their own lack of hope. They don't think escape's possible so it isn't.'

'And you feel you can trust God and go for it. Yeah, well...' He didn't know what to say, knew that nothing he said would stop his dad getting on that lift anyway. 'Do you want to start the book then?'

His father nodded, opened it carefully, smoothed down the tiny pages one by one as he turned them over. Then he began. ' "As I walked through the wilderness of this world, I lighted on a certain place where was a den, and laid me down in that place to sleep; and as I slept, I dreamed a dream. I dreamed, and behold..." '

Joe stared at his father as he read, determined to catch every word, willing the narrative to suck him in and make him forget what would be happening in just a few hours.

After lunch, Joe said, 'Dad, why don't you go when they deliver the food to the floor below, then come back when they collect the dirties? That way you wouldn't have to stay up there all night. What do you think?'

'You know why that wouldn't work, Joe. I have to wait up there until things have shut down for the night. Even at meal times there could be people working on the laundry or whatever else they do on that top floor. Plus there wouldn't be time for a look round.' He smiled. 'Don't worry, I'll be back for breakfast.'

Joe couldn't smile. He was thinking: you can't be sure of that. Anything could happen.

But he said nothing.

Supper was some kind of pasta, but Joe could hardly get anything down. His father seemed ravenous. As they heard the lifts begin the collecting routine he said, 'Last prayer before the off, okay, Joe?' Without waiting for the answer, he put his hands on Joe's, closed his eyes and said, 'Father, you know what we've been planning here. Now it's time to do it. Be with Joe as he stays here, Lord, and be with me as I go exploring.'

Joe didn't close his eyes, he kept them on his dad's face, saw the flush of excitement there. Would he have stopped him if he could? He only knew he was scared and wondered if his dad could feel his hands trembling.

Then his dad took off his belt and they stood by the hatch waiting for the bell.

Yes, there it was. Now, open the hatch, put the containers on, all as normal. Then instead of closing the hatch, his dad pushed the belt's prong into the catch on the cell wall. Immediately the lift began moving upwards.

It had worked.

They silently moved forward to look into the gaping hole which had appeared in the wall. Above, they could just make out the base of the lift moving away from them into the darkness. Then it was gone: all that was visible was a set of taut cables glistening in the cell's light. To left and right they could hear lifts gliding up and down, a bell ringing, then another.

His father looked excited. 'Just what I was hoping. You see, Joe, the darkness up there means there are doors on the kitchen hatches too – otherwise we'd see shafts of light coming down between the lifts. Now I know I can travel up and down without the risk of them seeing me.'

They waited, listened, kept looking up. Eventually, the base of the lift appeared again. They watched as it went past, saw the cables shudder as it stopped and heard the bell sound below them.

Joe felt his dad's arms go round him, such a quick hug he hardly had time to respond. Then his dad pushed himself up onto the hatch's ledge and lay along it, looking down, waiting. They heard the lift begin its ascent. Joe saw his father slide off the ledge. For one hideous moment it seemed he was falling into the darkness, but the timing was perfect and he was already getting into a sitting position as he vanished upwards.

Joe stared into the blackness. It was the first time he had been alone in the cell.

11

He continued staring until the whine of the lifts stopped and there was silence.

Now what? He looked at his CDs. Maybe later if he couldn't sleep. But for now he just wanted to be quiet, to be able to hear any sound that would give some clue as to what was happening up there.

He sat on his father's bed, on the edge at first, then right back, leaning against the wall. His hands were still trembling slightly, so he held them in front of his face willing them to stop. But they didn't. He let them drop into his lap.

He looked round the cell, trying to fill his mind with what he saw, trying to push out what he couldn't see but feared. Name what you see, Joe.

Floor. Ceiling with strip light. To the left, wall one. Door, air vent, toilet...

Air vent!

What if? His father had scoffed at the idea when Joe had mentioned it, but what if the cell was bugged? What if they'd heard all the conversations about the escape plan? What if, when Dad got on the lift, they were up there waiting to grab him? What would the punishment be? 'You not see son again! Different cells – for ever!' They could do it!

Joe covered his face with his hands, tried to remember word for word what his father had said. 'Why would they be listening to us? As far as they're concerned we're the Lost, the living dead. And think of the manpower – all these cells? No, Joe, we can say what we like, even about the Leader, and no one will know, no one will care.'

He rubbed his face with his hands, continued looking round the cell.

Opposite him, wall two. His own bed. CD player. CDs – one, two, three.

To the right, wall three. Hatch, the door folded into its bracket. A black hole, with a belt hanging beside it.

And, behind him, wall four. His dad's bed. Book: *Pilgrim's Progress*. He picked it up. Wow, the print was certainly tiny, too much work to read it now, later perhaps. Another book: the Bible.

Ah, bigger print here. His dad had been reading it most of the afternoon, somewhere around the middle. He opened it to about the right place. Psalms – what Dad had wanted to read with him until Joe had been sarcastic about David not having a clue what it felt like being locked up. He knew at the time that what he'd said was unfair, but he just wanted to stop his dad coming up with any of his so-easy-to-say 'God Understands' statements.

But things were different now. He didn't need to blame God for what had happened. He knew who the real villain was now: it was the Leader who'd got them into this, not God. Over the last days, weeks, he'd been brought, through his dad's readings, face-to-face with a God who really did care, who may stretch people, like Joseph, but in the end wouldn't let them down.

And God was the same today. He could see that with his dad. He'd never doubted that God would work things out in his own way, in his own time. Joe had seen the excitement on his dad's face before he went up on the lift, not mad desperation, but total confidence in someone more powerful than this prison and the people who built it.

He looked down at the open Bible and read the first verses his eyes settled on: 'I wait patiently for God to save me; I depend on him alone. He alone protects and saves me; he is my defender, and I shall never be defeated.'

And something inside him said: yes, that's right. If God was on your side, how could anyone, even the Leader, defeat you? God is God after all.

His eyes caught the start of the previous psalm, 61: 'Hear my cry, O God; listen to my prayer! In despair and far from home I call to you!'

And he remembered Joseph in his cell: far from home certainly, but knowing he was never far from God. So he'd called, and God, yes, at the right time, had answered.

God.

Joe breathed the word into the air of the cell.

God.

A God who listened. A God who answered. A God who could help.

He sat still for a long moment, couldn't get away from the fact that he'd be totally stupid to ignore that kind of offer. He closed his eyes, breathed in and began: 'God, I've not done this before, not recently anyway. But you see what's happening here and I want to pray for my dad. He's up there and he needs your help.'

He stopped. Something was wrong. He wasn't getting through. And he knew why. Traitors can't pray. Traitors can't expect favours from those they betray. And Joe was a traitor. A Judas. A Raymond. He'd put himself outside the circle. His own choice.

Then some words of his dad's came into his mind: 'Joe, you can remake that choice. Anytime. That's why Jesus died – to keep the door open.'

Joe knew what he had to do. He had to reach forward, take hold of the handle of that door, open it wide and step into God's presence. Then he could be forgiven. Then he could be heard.

He sat, hardly breathing. Then he lifted his hand and reached out. He knew there was nothing there, but in another sense he knew something very real was there. He knew he was on the brink of touching a very real door, of coming into the presence of a very real God.

He took hold of the handle. And stopped.

Wait, Joe, he told himself. Wait. Remember your questions. Do you believe in God, really believe, or is it just that you're alone and scared and clutching at straws?

And he answered himself: I believe. I always have, deep down, even when I was speaking to Mr Webb that day, even when we were put in here. And, yeah, I am scared, but, no, it's not just that. I believe in God. I believe Jesus is the way to him.

But, Joe, do you really want him, this Jesus, in your life? Will you want him when – if – you get out of here? When you're with Anna, your mates?

And he answered: Yes, I do want him. I can't go on living a lie. If Anna thinks I'm daft – tough. This is what I want.

So he pushed the door fully open and went forward.

After a few moments, he opened his eyes and looked around. All the same: four walls, black hole where the hatch had been. But all different too. He glanced down at the Bible again, Psalm 63, first verse 'O God, you are my God...' Yeah, not just Dad's God now. My God. My saviour. My helper. No matter what.

He closed his eyes, began to pray again. Now the words came easily, poured out. He told God how sorry he was to have pushed him away, for going along with the Leader, with the crowd. He told him his fears for his father, for the next night, for the future. Then he remembered how his father had prayed for other Christians in prison, so he prayed for any in the cells around, and for those he remembered from that web site and from that man's visit to the church.

When he had finished, he put the Bible on the floor, lay down on his father's bed and fell immediately asleep.

He woke up and wondered why he was on the wrong bed. Then it all came back to him. He grinned, sat up and said aloud, 'Thank you, Lord, that you're here.'

He crossed to the space in the wall and gazed up into the darkness. At that moment, the cell light came on to full strength and, as he continued to look up, he became aware, little by little, of distant noises, then eventually the whirring of the lifts began. He could see the cables close to him shimmering in the cell's light as they moved up and down. It was easy to distinguish the sound of their lift from the ones to left and right, easy to count the journeys it was making.

Now it's at the third floor down, now it's going up… fourth floor down, up… fifth floor down, up. We're next! Would Dad be on top of it? Of course there'd be no way he could get into the cell on this trip but – yes! Here it was!

The lift shuddered to a stop. The bell rang by his ear. Then…

Two knocks, hardly audible, from the top of the lift! He was there all right! Joe couldn't reach up to knock back so he grabbed one of the food containers and thumped it against the top.

With a chill he realised he'd done the wrong thing. Officially, the hatch wasn't open. Upstairs they'd be wondering why he hadn't opened it. Could they have heard the thump? Probably not, but even so… He shoved the container back in its slot and grabbed at the belt, pulling the prong from the catch. Then, as quickly as he could, he unloaded the containers, hoisted the used toilet bucket into its slot and pushed the prong back into the catch.

He watched, panting. The lift started to move upwards again.

'Thanks, Lord, thanks.'

He stood there biting his lip. Eventually, the lift began its next downward journey. This time he'd see his dad, help pull him out.

He stared up into the blackness. Come on, lift, come on.

And there it was, sliding down towards him. He stepped back. Its base appeared in the wall space, then the inside of the lift with the containers for the cell below, then the top.

Then… yes! Dad!

But as soon as Joe saw him, he knew that something had gone dreadfully wrong.

12

It was like his dad had gone through a time warp and come back twenty years older. His face was grey and his movements were slow and clumsy as he clambered into the cell. But what Joe noticed most were his fingers. The tips had been bleeding and the nails were broken. As they hugged, he wondered what had happened up there. But he was back, that was the main thing.

'Come on, Dad, sit down on your bed. What do you want – eat first or wash?'

His father looked at him blankly. 'What? Oh, I'd better wash. Look at these hands.'

Joe didn't like to say he couldn't stop looking at them. He just brought one of the hot water containers over to him and said, 'Want me to—'

'No, Joe, I'm fine. Or I will be in a few minutes.'

Joe took a few sideways glances at him as he stripped and had an all-over wash. No, he was okay. Just the fingers.

Joe began to open the food containers.

'How did you get on down here?' his dad asked.

'Fine. Yeah, fine. Slept really well.' Joe wasn't sure why he didn't want to tell him what had happened, about reaching out for the door, about his prayer. It just didn't seem the right time, it was too important to talk about between mouthfuls of porridge. 'Are you okay, I mean, holding the spoon?'

'Yes, Joe. They're not that bad. I've done more damage kicking myself. I should have thought— oh, let's finish this first, then I'll tell you. And as for the question you're dying to ask: are we going tonight? The answer's yes, you bet.'

'I just didn't think it through. There I was jumping with joy that there were doors on the hatches – and not giving a thought as to how I'd open them from this side. It was pitch black up there, the light from here got lost after a couple of floors. It was black and hot. But then one of the kitchen staff opened the hatch, which gave a little bit of light round the edge of the lift and meant I could stand up safely. There was a lot of noise coming from the kitchen so I reckoned they wouldn't hear me. I found I could easily reach up to the hatch above, but then they closed the hatch in the kitchen and I lost my light. So I waited till the place was quiet, gave it about another hour, then got to work. I guess I dreamt I could just slide the door along in its slot. But it didn't budge a fraction.

'So I sat down for a rest. Because I was a bit away from the front wall, I noticed it – a tiny gleam of light coming from the laundry hatch three lifts over to the right. It looked like it wasn't shut properly.

'That's when it became hairy. Because I knew there was a gap, a bit less than a metre, I'd say, between the lifts. And that gap went all the way down. I didn't think about it, I just prayed and went for it and jumped out into the darkness. It wasn't far to jump, I was just afraid of losing my balance or getting the direction wrong in the dark. But I made it. Then the second and third jumps were easy. That light was by my head now, a thin triangle. I think the hatch door hadn't been put on dead straight so it wouldn't close properly.

'I tried to get my fingers in the crack to push it across. You can see how I tried. But they were too thick and I had nothing else I could use. So all I could do was jump back and sit it out.'

Joe looked round the cell, grinned and said, 'Shams to the rescue!' He picked up one of the CD cases and snapped an edge off the lid. 'This do?' He held up the piece of plastic. 'I reckon it's pretty tough.'

'Genius, absolute genius. But I knew we'd come up with something. Now look, I'm dying for a sleep. Can we just have a quick prayer together first?'

Joe wanted to pray too but as soon as his dad finished, he stretched out on his bed, said, 'Wake me for lunch,' and fell straight asleep.

Joe sat on his own bed, looking at him. So, they were going tonight. With their bit of plastic. But what were they going to find when they got the hatch open? It was still all ifs and buts, and still full of risks. New ones too. He wasn't sure he fancied this jumping about in the dark. Not that he was afraid of heights, he'd conquered that fear during the rock climbing sessions in School 3. But that was in the light. And there was someone above holding the safety rope. Tonight, no light, no rope.

And what if they got out? What then? He hadn't liked to ask Dad as he was afraid there wouldn't be any answer. They couldn't go home, that was for sure. Some friend's attic? For how long? He sighed. Too much to think about.

Silently he reached for the Bible on the floor by his dad's bed, and opened it to the contents page. Most of the book names were mysteries to him. So what about Acts? Sounded more inviting than Obadiah or Lamentations. Let's go for it.

For over an hour he read, occasionally glancing up at his father lightly snoring on the opposite bed. It was a thrilling book all right. But Joe found it was more than that: it was... real. The stories were more than stories, it was as if he was in them, like he was there in the courtroom when Peter was refusing to keep quiet about Jesus, like he was there with Paul hiking over the mountains of southern Turkey. He could identify with these characters, because they'd all gone through the same experience: making that decision to follow Jesus, opening the door to him. He, Joe Collins, was part of that long chain of believers that reached from the days of the Bible to the present. So what he and his dad were going through could be Acts, chapter two million and two or something. The story was still going on. And God was still going on, the same now as then.

When he'd finished the book, he turned back and read one part again. Peter was in prison for his faith, chained between soldiers, due to go to court the next day. Then – flash, bang – an angel appeared and led him out to freedom. Just a short time before, Joe would have sneered at the story, said something like, 'Oh yeah, very likely. Can't see any angel here at the moment, Dad. Perhaps he'll come down with the laundry.' But now he saw nothing to sneer at, he knew God was God and could send an angel to them just as easily as to Peter. But God chose how he was going to work it, and when. And, Joe thought with a smile, just as Peter knew where to go when he got out, so would they.

'Help me trust you, Lord, whatever happens.'

But over lunch he couldn't hold the question back.

'After we get out, Joe? Oh, I've thought about it all right, just didn't want to talk about things too far ahead in case – well, you know what I mean. I think the best plan is to head down to Wilfham on the Kent coast. Bernie's got a cottage there. You remember Bernie, big and bearded, he and his wife always used to go down there on a Friday evening so they could spend Saturday on their boat and come back in time for church. Well, I'm banking on him still doing it. I know he's travelled a lot so I'm hoping he knows someone abroad who can help. Yeah, I know nothing's sure, but if God gets us out, his plan won't stop there.'

Joe nodded. Just what he'd been reading. Slowly it was dawning on him that escape was a real possibility. This could actually be their last day in this hole. Yes!

They were perched on the ledge, Joe on the right, his father on the left. The prisoner below would be loading up his empty supper containers. Joe took a look round the cell. The beds, the CD player, the broken case, the Bible – Dad had tucked the little *Pilgrim's Progress* in the top pocket of his shirt but the Bible was too big.

A click, a whirring noise. The cables shivered. The lift began to move up towards them.

'Feet first, Joe, then fall forward onto your hands and knees. Now!'

And they were kneeling beside each other gliding upwards into the darkness.

'Joe, feel where the side edge is. Then get into a sitting position. Careful now, try not to touch the cables.'

All easier said than done. He hadn't expected it to be this dark. The cell light had been on all the time and he just wasn't used to having his eyes open and seeing nothing. He reached sideways with his right hand. Further. Further. There. The edge of the lift: hard smooth metal, then – nothing. He pulled his hand back, aware he was beginning to sweat, then eased himself into a sitting position facing the doors and tried to sit still.

A dim glow appeared above them to the right, then one to the left – light squeezing round the lifts where the kitchen hatches had been opened. He looked across to where he knew his father was. Yes, he could just see his outline if he stared hard. The lift continued upwards, passing the patches of light, then stopped. He could hear the clamour of the kitchen now and what might have been someone laughing.

It was hot, so hot. He could feel the stickiness in his armpits.

Then someone in the kitchen opened the hatch. He could feel the vibration as the door slid across. Now that someone was unloading the containers. His head would be only centimetres away from Joe's feet.

Still, Joe, keep them still…

A drop of sweat trickled down his forehead. He wiped it away with a finger. Then more came so he just closed his eyes and let them run down his face. This was awful: the heat, the need to be totally quiet, the sheer drop only an arm's length away. God, please help.

Despite the heat, he was beginning to shiver. He felt

his dad patting him gently on his arm, the fingers saying: it's all right, it's going fine.

The trembling was stopping now. He let himself relax a little.

After a while, he didn't know how long, he heard a whisper, 'Joe, sit up slowly. Mind the cable, it's quite close to your face.' He blinked his eyes open and realised that his head had been resting on his father's shoulder. He sat up. 'Now inch yourself back so you're leaning against the back wall. Do you see that tiny strip of light up there now?'

'Mmm? Oh, yes. Seems a long way over.'

'Three jumps over. Are you ready?'

'Now?'

'I think you slept a bit. It's been quiet in the kitchen for ages. We can't wait too long.'

'Slept? I… oh yeah, I'm ready.'

But he wasn't, probably never would be. He had felt the nothingness over the side of the lift and he was afraid of it. And it was so dark.

'Right. Now edge round the cable. Put your right hand out, find mine. Good. Now stand up. You're at the front of the lift, facing the jump. Feel the wall with your left hand. Now, move your left foot forward till you find the edge.'

'Okay.' He could feel his lips trembling as he said the word. He had never felt this frightened, ever.

'Joe, listen to me. It's not a big jump. You can do it, no problem. You hear me? *No problem.* Forget the gap. Think of it as jumping over a puddle. Keep your toe at the edge, use the hand on the wall to get the direction right, push off hard, and there's *no problem.* I'll go first. Let go of my hand now.'

Joe felt a slight rush of air and then heard his dad land on the top of the next lift.

'See, Joe, it's easy, even for an old man like me. Now, when you're ready.'

Go on, Joe, don't fail him now. Don't fail yourself. Go on!

He breathed in hard, pushed down with his left foot and kicked out with the right.

But he knew, even as he jumped, that he wasn't going to make it, knew that at the vital moment something inside him had cried out, 'No!' The muscles had tensed and the momentum had gone. He felt the ball of the foot land on the edge of the next lift but his body, instead of continuing forwards, was beginning to fall backwards, his other foot still hanging over the chasm.

He slapped his hand onto the wall on his left. But it was smooth and featureless, there was nothing to grab hold of.

It was like sitting down. Only there was no chair beneath him. Just a black gulf, seven storeys deep. And there was nothing he could do to stop himself dropping into it.

13

He tried to scream. But he had no breath for it.

His hand squeaked against the wall as he struggled to stop his body sliding down. His foot clung desperately to its perch.

But neither hand nor foot were any use.

He was going…

Then something smacked him hard on his right side. It felt like the skin was being squeezed in a vice. For a moment he was totally still, stuck to the wall like a swatted fly. Then came a thump behind his shoulder, another vice-like grip. He heard his father breathe in hard and felt the downward slide reversed. Now he was sliding *up* the wall, as if the foot on the edge of the lift was a hinge. Up and over. He fell in a heap on the lift's roof and hit the cable with his shoulder.

Then his father's arms were lifting him up again, hauling him into a crouch, then into a standing position.

'Listen, Joe, we're not waiting long enough for you to think about what nearly happened there. We're jumping again. Two steps forward. Good. Now feel the edge like before. And the wall. Got it? Good. Now: *jump*!'

And Joe sprang with all the energy he possessed, no

holding back. Almost immediately, he felt the roof of the next lift under his feet. He heard his dad land beside him, straightaway felt his hand on his back.

'Great! Now, do it again. Foot. Hand. *Jump!*'

He didn't think, he just obeyed. Yes! He was there! Three jumps! He waved his fists in triumph.

Then his dad was holding him by the shoulders.

'Sit down, Joe, take deep breaths.'

He didn't need to be told – his legs had suddenly gone to rubber underneath him, and he slid down, feeling light-headed and giggly.

'Breathe in… out.'

Finally he was able to say, 'How did you manage to grab me like that?'

'I heard your hand sliding down the wall, could just make out your outline, so I lunged out and pulled.'

'Wow.'

'Thank God, I'd say. Now come on, stand up – we've got work to do.'

Joe could hear his dad getting the strip of plastic from his pocket, could see it being slid into the tiny triangle of light by his head and moved from side to side.

'It's shifting, Dad. You go to the top of the crack, I think I can get my fingers in the bottom.'

'Yes, boss.'

A few seconds later, they slid the hatch door open.

'Anyone there, Dad?'

'Bit late to think about that now. Though come to think of it, they'd probably have died of shock, seeing the hatch open and my smiling face appearing. Joe, be ready to give me a push up if I need it.'

But he was up and over with no trouble. Joe followed.

They'd made it. The laundry room.

A row of dimmed strip lights in the ceiling showed them a large, almost empty room. Joe gazed round: how odd to be *seeing* it at last. There was the dentist's chair, pushed against the left-hand wall. Along the longer wall opposite was a series of closed doors: the three on the left had glass panels showing the rooms beyond were in darkness – offices? Then came the passenger lift, a door he presumed led to the staircase, and at the far end the electronically controlled doors leading to the room where they'd been blindfolded.

His eyes continued round. Against the right hand wall were two stacks of chairs, a table and a pile of large plastic baskets. Then in the corner to his immediate right sat a huge grey metal box – the washing machine? Joe moved towards it – yes, there were the dials. A pipe led from the back of the machine and disappeared through a hole near the ceiling. A little further along the wall at the same height as the hole was a large metal grating. Then began the long block of supply lifts – seven, Joe counted – they'd come through the hatch of number three.

His father pointed upwards. 'That's it then. That's our chance.'

The grating. The weak point. The space behind had to lead to that chimney – all part of some kind of air-conditioning system probably, with a machine somewhere pushing the air round.

Without needing to be told, Joe silently went over to the chairs, eased one from its stack and placed it below the grating. His father stood on it, his head now level with the grating, which he looked through left and right. Then he put his hands at its bottom two corners and gently pushed. It immediately lifted away from the wall. He let it fall into his arms, stood it beside him on the chair, and used the other hand to explore the exposed space. He nodded down to Joe and twisted the grating back through its slot, pushing it along to the left.

So, there was a floor to the space. It was like a little tunnel up there. Great.

His father heaved himself up. Joe saw his body disappear to the right, behind the block of lifts.

He waited, aware of the faint whirring noise of the air-conditioning coming from the opening.

Come on, Dad...

It seemed an eternity, but it could only have been seconds before he saw his father nodding down to him. Joe climbed on the chair and his dad helped pull him up into the tunnel. He felt round with his hands. As he'd expected, it was the same plastic material as the cell, the walls curving as they met ceiling and floor but high enough to crouch or sit in. It was dark though, the light coming up from the laundry hardly helped at all. But there, a little way beyond his father, was a pool of grey light coming into the tunnel from above. It could only mean one thing: the chimney. The way out.

Then they both realised it at once. The chair. It would give them away as soon as one of the guards came into the room. They could replace the grating, but the chair would still scream out: 'Escape! They went this way!' It could cut their time to get away by hours. It couldn't stay there.

But there was no way they could reach it. They were up here. The chair was down there. They gazed at it with dismay.

Then his dad said, 'Joe, I'm going to back up. Get on your stomach with your shoulders by the opening.'

Joe knew what he was thinking. 'But is there room up here for it, Dad?'

'There's got to be, Joe, even if we have to break it into bits with our bare hands.'

With his dad pressing on his ankles, Joe began wriggling head first through the opening. But even with his hips on the edge and his body twisted so his right hand swung below him, he still couldn't reach the chair. Not even brush the top of it.

'I'll try it the other way round, Dad.' He turned over so that he was sitting by the opening with his back to it. 'Keep hold of the ankles, okay?' Then he twisted himself out and uncurled his body backwards. Yes, he could reach it now, get both hands on it, but the back of the chair was plastic and not easy to grip. The last thing he wanted was the chair skating across the floor out of reach.

His father let him drop a few more centimetres. Yes! He clamped a hand on each side and lifted it off the floor. For a moment or two he just dangled there. Then he realised he was stuck. He'd had the idea of gripping the chair to his chest, then curling his body back towards the hole, like a vertical press-up, but it was impossible. It wasn't just the weight, though his shoulders were beginning to ache. It was also that his hands were getting sweaty and he was losing his grip: he still couldn't get his hands *under* anything.

'Please, God,' he murmured, 'help me lift it. Don't let it slip.'

But as he finished the prayer he felt the chair doing just that – sliding little by little through his fingers. He let it down on the floor as quietly as he could and pulled himself up.

They sat either side of the opening, gazing down.

'All I can think, Joe, is for one of us to go down and put it back. But then to get up here again, you'd have to use a chair.'

'What if I went down and put it back, then you leaned out as far as you could and caught me as I jumped up—'

'We'd both end up in a heap on the floor. No, Joe, we'll just have to—'

'Dad – my belt! That's it! Help me get down.'

In a few seconds he was back on the floor, tying his belt round the chair's back panel, letting the rest of it drape over the top. Great – now when he was lowered down, he could wind that loose part round his wrist and haul the chair up without the risk of dropping it. Good job he'd listened to his dad and, like him, kept the belt, the 'tacky little strip of plastic' he remembered calling it. Both belts had been crucial.

But why had God made this chair business so complicated? Why hadn't he just given him the extra strength?

Then, just as he was about to climb back up, he saw, and smiled. So, was that why? They hadn't thought of that, and they certainly wouldn't have noticed it from up there, it would have been out of sight…

'Dad,' he whispered up. 'You know what we forgot?'

And without waiting for an answer he went and closed (or as near to closed as it went) the hatch to lift number three. Which, if God had said yes to Joe's prayer, they would have left gaping open. Which, in turn, would have set the guards thinking, and looking, and… Joe breathed a thank you into the silence of the room. God really did see all.

Five minutes later they were sitting on the right of the opening, the chair was on its back on the left. It hadn't been the most elegant of manoeuvres. Joe had thumped himself and his dad with the chair several times, and there was a nasty moment when they couldn't get the last leg of it though the opening because one of Joe's legs was in the way. But they'd done it, and the grating had fitted back easily. Now they began to crawl their way towards the pool of grey light.

Soon they were sitting looking up through the grating at the base of the chimney. Looking at the sky. The sight of it made Joe's heart pound. Freedom, five metres above him, maybe less. So close now…

His father lifted the grating off its supports and placed it silently on the tunnel floor behind him. They stood together, their top halves in the chimney. Then they looked at its sides.

What had they expected? A ladder? How stupid.

The grim reality was a smooth surface all the way round. That same plastic stuff, no grip to it. And no cracks either, so no finger or footholds. Five metres, probably less. So near and yet so far.

They stood in silence. Further along the tunnel, the whirring noise continued.

Finally his dad said, 'If you stood on my shoulders, maybe there's a chance.'

Joe shrugged. Surely it was too high? But they had to try something. He put a foot in his father's cupped hands and was lifted up, up… Then, steadying himself with his hands on the chimney's sides, he put his feet on his father's shoulders, pushed his hands towards the rim. No, nowhere near. Then he felt hands being pushed under his feet and hoisting him further. Surely now…

His fingers clawed at the plastic. He was about half a metre short. His father let him down.

'Anyway, Dad, what if I *had* reached it? How were *you* going to get up? I could have asked at that stately home for a rope, I guess, but…'

A rope.

Joe remembered back to last year. He was in a harness, with a rope attached to it, the rope snaking all the way up the cliff face to the instructor at the top. Not a real cliff face but the one at School 3 which the Leader had ordered to be built. The instructor was shouting down, 'Here's the chimney, Collins. You remember me telling you how to tackle it, I hope.' Yes, he did.

And he still did. 'A chimney, Collins, is a cleft in a rock face. You use your whole body to climb it. You lean your back on one side of the cleft, put your feet flat on the other. You push your hands against the rock behind you and slide your body up a few centimetres. Then you get your feet to follow. One foot at a time though, Collins. Ha ha. First your body, then your feet. Keep the pressure up all the time. Easy.'

Easy. Yes, it was then. With boots and special gloves and rough surfaces for them to grip onto. And with someone above you holding the rope. None of that here.

But it might still be possible. He stopped.

For just that moment he'd forgotten. There was still the same problem. His dad. He would have to do it too.

'Dad,' he whispered.

'Joe, your face is an open book. You've got an idea, something you learnt doing PSA, I bet, then you realised there's a problem. I guess the problem's me. Am I right?'

He sighed. 'Right on all counts, Dad.' He explained the idea.

'Well, I'll give it a try. I can't believe God's brought us all this way just for a glimpse of sky. So let's go.'

Right. Joe sighed, ran his hands down the wall. So smooth. But it was the only way.

He pushed his back against the wall and hooked his arms so the palms were flat against it by his waist. It pulled his shoulders away from the wall a bit but that couldn't be helped. He kicked up with his left foot, placed it hard against the opposite wall of the tunnel, also at waist level. Now the moment of truth. Would the walls be too smooth to hold him up? Gingerly he lifted his right foot from the floor, raised it slowly, placed it alongside.

His body stayed in position though he could feel his own weight pulling him down, like the floor had suddenly become magnetic. And his legs being almost at full stretch wasn't ideal – but as the tunnel curved inwards slightly before joining the chimney, after a few moves it should get easier.

'Okay, Joe?'

'Yeah.' Except he hadn't started. Come on, Joe, move! he told himself. This isn't like jumping about on lifts – you've done this before. And you can see what you're doing.

But the magnet in the floor was getting stronger every moment.

Right.

Go.

He took a deep breath, pushed his hands hard against the wall behind him and slid his body up.

Now the feet: one… two. Squeaked a bit, but they stayed.

Yes! We have lift off!

Go, rocketboy! Hands: push. Body: lift. Feet: walk. And again. And again…

Now he was level with the roof of the tunnel, about to enter the chimney.

Hands: push. Body: lift. Feet: walk. Again.

And into the chimney. Yes, easier now. Again.

He glanced below him. His dad was swinging his legs up now, getting into the start position. He had to bend his legs that bit more than Joe, less of a stretch. Good. Again.

He was beginning to be aware of a slight ache in his calf muscles now but he could cope with that. And his hands were getting sweaty. Making sure his back was jammed against the wall, he wiped them on his jeans.

And again.

'How you doing, Dad?'

'Well, it's harder than press-ups.'

Again.

Halfway? Nearly. Just keep going, Joe. Hands, body, feet. Keep going.

But with every move that pain in his legs was getting worse – it had spread up to his thighs now. It was the effort of having to keep up so much pressure. Real rock, or even fake School 3 rock, would give a bit of grip. This was squeaky smooth.

Again.

No, he couldn't. He'd have to rub his legs. Carefully he eased the right leg away from the wall, brought his right hand towards it.

It was too much for the left leg to cope with. Immediately it began sliding down. In a second the pressure keeping him up would be gone.

His dad saw what was happening, slid his own left foot upwards, shoved it underneath Joe's, stopped the slide. Joe slammed his other foot back onto the wall.

Nearly…

'Shouldn't try that too often, Joe.'

'Thanks for the advice, Dad. And for the foot.' He screwed his eyes shut, tried to ignore the pain. Both his legs were trembling now. But there was no choice.

Hands. Body. Feet. Again… Again…

No, he couldn't do any more. A metre to the top, maybe a metre and a half. Impossible. A kind of numbness seemed to be spreading over the lower part of his back, and when he took his hands away from the wall they were shaking like crazy.

'Go on, Joe. Not far.'

No. Can't. He looked up, the grey circle of sky was occupying so much more of his field of vision now. Yes. Must. He pushed his hands back as hard as he could against the cold plastic, but nothing happened. His body just wouldn't slide up.

Just then, something moved in the greyness above him. A bird flying across. Just a bird. But it sent a bolt of electricity through him. It was free. And Joe could be free if he covered that last metre and a half.

He pushed again, aware of a strange noise emerging from his throat, aware of his whole body vibrating with the strain. He couldn't consciously pray, but something deep inside him was crying out for strength.

And his back peeled away from the wall and lifted itself up a few centimetres before slamming back.

Now the feet.

He stared at them, willed the left one to move. And it did, wriggling, wormlike, up the wall. The right one followed.

Again.

Again.

Yes… yes… the bird… free… free, Joe, free…

Again.

Again.

And he was there, his feet sticking up over the rim of the chimney.

He could see the tops of trees. He could feel a breeze on his face.

He began to cry, not tears, but deep down in his throat, a gentle throbbing.

'Joe… listen to me.'

His father. Just below him. He could hear the pain in his voice. A rasping. Like he was dying.

'Joe… get one… hand over… feel how wide… can you sit…?'

Slowly he took his right hand from the wall, moved his arm over the rim, slapped the hand down. He couldn't feel the outer edge.

'Yes, there's room to sit. But I can't get there. I'd have to take my feet off the wall.' With that hand on the rim, he was already stretched to the limit, his legs dead straight in order to keep up the pressure.

For a long moment, all Joe could hear was their heavy breathing. Then his dad's voice came again – he didn't sound so bad now, more natural.

'Joe, I'm going to swivel round, get at right angles to you so you can use me as a bridge… Okay, I'm right under you now. I've jammed myself in as hard as I can. Put as much weight on your right arm as possible, then drop your legs onto mine and slide across and up. Understand?'

Joe understood the idea all right, but he understood the danger too. If he put too much weight on his father's legs, he'd send him crashing to his death. But there seemed no choice. Slowly, he lowered his right leg till it rested on his father's knees. He knew he could only hold this position for a moment, so he quickly brought the other leg down, grabbed at the rim with his left hand and pulled himself across. His dad's shoes were beginning to slide. So, as fast as he could, he heaved himself up onto the rim, taking the pressure off his dad.

He was in time. The slide stopped. His dad quickly worked his feet back up, then put both hands on the rim. Being that bit taller than Joe, his legs still reached the opposite wall. He heaved himself up and in a moment they were sitting together at the top of the chimney, legs dangling into the darkness.

Joe breathed in. Fresh air. It actually smelt of something, he'd never noticed that before. Of earth, trees and flowers. It was beautiful, just magic. He relished its coolness reaching down into his lungs. His whole body was tingling with pleasure.

'Careful now, Joe. Swing your legs over. Keep hold of the rim with your hands.'

It was about two metres to the ground. They dropped down. The earth was soft, the grass damp. Joe wanted to roll about in it, burying his face in the grass and pushing his fingers into the earth.

He might have done it. But then the siren started – a low-pitched wailing coming up the chimney. It took them a moment to realise what had happened: when they had landed on the ground, they had set off an alarm.

'Joe! Run!'

But then they saw light spilling up the steps and a figure emerging from the prison.

It was a guard. He had reached the top of the steps now. And he had seen them. They gazed in horror as he raised his gun.

14

Joe had never known a bleaker moment. All that agonizing effort, all those frights, those risks – for nothing. They'd just be marched down to the cell again – or... separated... *no, no, please God, no...*

But what was happening?

The guard was still pointing his gun at them, but it was as if his battery had run out. He just stood there, silent, unmoving.

It was his father who moved first. But what was he doing? Without taking his eyes off the guard, he was pulling something from his shirt pocket, the now crumpled copy of *Pilgrim's Progress*, and holding it out in front of him like a shield. But how could a tiny book protect you from a bullet? Did his dad think it would act like some kind of magic charm? Surely not. What then?

All three of them were totally still. The siren had stopped, the only sound now the soft swish of the breeze through the treetops.

Then came a voice. Someone in the laundry room was shouting up the steps: 'Anything?'

The silent guard lowered his gun a fraction and Joe began to understand what was happening. For he could see now it was the guard with fair hair, the one who'd said, 'It's lunch soon', the one who Joe was sure had sent them the book his dad was holding in front of him.

Another moment of total stillness.

Then the guard glanced towards the steps and shouted back, 'No. Nothing. A fox maybe.' And, pushing the gun back into his belt, he too pulled something from his pocket and laid it on the grass in front of him. Then he pointed to the trees over Joe's right shoulder, looked at his father and gave one brief nod – maybe even a smile. Joe couldn't be sure.

Then he was gone, down the steps and through the door. They heard the whirring as it slid across, the light fading, then dying.

Joe's dad pushed the book back in his pocket and crossed to where the guard had stood. He picked up what he had left and showed it to Joe. Money, a bundle of Euro notes.

'You were right, Joe. He *was* a friend. Even pointed to the best route out. Come on, we'd better go.'

They began running towards the trees.

'Got lost, did you?' The driver turned to them and grinned.

Joe saw there was a smile on his father's face too as he answered. 'Yes, you could say that.'

They had seen the van's headlights as they climbed over the low wall. Joe had thought they were never coming to the end of the trees, but then there was the wall, the road – and the van. And there was his dad, running into the road, waving his arms. It was good the driver had agreed to give them a lift straightaway: Joe wondered what his dad might have done if he'd said no.

'Sort of night walk, was it? Bit of adventure? Well, you seem happy but, if you don't mind me saying, you don't seem very well prepared. I mean, I know there's a moon, but you still need a torch. You've got no water bottle either, big mistake that. Heavy, I know, but—'

'Look, we're in a real hurry. We need to get to Wilfham. If I paid you – I've got these Euros – you couldn't take us all the way, could you?'

The driver glanced across at them, then at the money. His smile was even broader now. 'Well, I can see you're father and son so I can guess what's in your mind: the lady of the house is going to get pretty worried unless we get you home fast. So, yeah, sure. I'm going down to the coast anyway, so it isn't too far out of my way. Glad to be of service.'

An hour later they were sitting eating fried egg sandwiches in Bernie's front room.

'It's an amazing story. When I saw you at the door, I thought I was still asleep, couldn't believe it. Now I've heard what happened, well!' He laughed. 'But I sure praise God for dreams like this!' He turned to his wife, sitting smiling beside him. 'Here, love, don't I get an egg sandwich too, to get me over the shock?'

He spent much of the next hour on the phone in his study. When he came back his sense of relief was obvious.

'Yes, it's all working out. There's a boat at six, gets into Calais an hour later. I've reserved tickets, got to pick them up by 5.30. François Darnel, good man, known him for years, he'll be there to meet the boat, wearing a yellow jumper, he said, so you can pick him out. He's the pastor of a church in Lille. You can trust him completely. I told him enough for him to know how important it is. He'll decide whether to keep you there or send you on, and he'll decide what to do with the information you give him. He's on the ball politically, knows one or two people who can get things moving.'

'Moving?'

'I think, Andy, if this is handled right, it could well be the beginning of the end for the Leader. Once the human rights organisations hear about these prisons, he won't know what's hit him. And I'm sure governments will get involved. They've turned a blind eye up to now, but this'll be too much for them to stomach. On top of that, when people hear that their loved ones aren't dead like they were told, that the Lost have just been… *found*, well, can you imagine the uproar? Even those who cheer loudest at the annual processions are going to feel a bit sick. Now, don't want to rush you, but we need to pray, then we need to drive.'

Joe sat at the back of Bernie's car, looking at the drizzle in the car park's lights. A few minutes before, Bernie had told them, 'I'll collect the tickets as they're in my name. Good job you don't need passports for France these days. Now you stay here, neither of you look a bundle of health, especially in my old sweaters, and we don't want to attract too much attention.'

Then he'd got his bulky frame out of the car, crossed to the ferry building and disappeared through the door marked 'Departures'.

Departures. They'd made it. Soon they would go through that door and… depart.

Other people were making for that door, most of them carrying cases. One young couple stopped every few steps despite the rain and wrapped their arms round each other. Which one of them was 'departing'? Joe wondered. The boy, by the look of the luggage. His mind went to Anna – it would've been nice if she'd been here to say goodbye, he thought. Then his view of the couple was blocked by a man in a raincoat. He was heading for the same door but he had no luggage. Suddenly a gust of wind blew across the car park and the man's open raincoat billowed out behind him and began flapping.

Flapping… like the wings of a bird of prey.

Joe felt a violent shudder shoot through his body. For he'd seen that man before. On a beach, coming towards them. Wearing that same raincoat. It was the Vulture.

15

He nudged his father, pointed a shaking finger at the man. 'Dad, it's him...'

'Who, Joe? What do you mean? Bernie? Why are you looking like that?'

'The man on the beach who arrested us. It's him. There.'

'I can't see...'

But then a woman waved across the car park and the Vulture turned towards her. Joe saw his face for the first time. He was smiling, now he was kissing the woman on the cheek, now they were going together towards the entrance... It wasn't the Vulture at all. Just a man in a raincoat.

'Joe: listen. I think things like this are going to happen for a while. We're going to see those guards, those soldiers, coming round corners, bumping into us, all around. Every man in a raincoat that isn't done up is going to be that man on the beach. But, Joe, it never will be. When we get on that boat, that's it. No Raymond will be able to give us away, no Tracker will be able to locate us. We'll be safe for as long as it takes.'

Then Bernie was getting back in the car. 'All's fine. Here are your tickets. It's boarding now. Look, here's some extra cash, don't argue, you'll need it. Though I know François and the other Christians over there will see you all right. So – ready?'

The drizzle stopped as they boarded the boat, so they sat in solitude on the wooden benches out on deck. They sky and sea were both grey, it was just possible to see where one stopped and the other began.

'Dad, what made that guard take the job in the first place? If he's a Christian, and I guess he must be—'

'Perhaps it was like the situation with Raymond and he reckoned he had too much to lose if he didn't take it. Or perhaps the Leader's mob had some hold on him. I don't know.'

'So then, why did he let us escape like that?'

'Sometimes, Joe, God brings us to a crunch point. Everything that guard believed deep down came to the surface. I believe God prompted me to show him that book and I think it revived memories for him, of a time when he wanted to be a pilgrim too. And it's possible he's got a son at home your age. Whatever, he came to that crunch point, and he did what God wanted.'

'Yeah… Dad, listen. Talking of crunch points, I-I've got something very important to tell you. I should have told you before, I guess, but it was hard to find the right moment.' He was beginning to shiver.

'Want to go inside, Joe?'

He shook his head, so his father put his arm round his shoulders.

'Go on, then.'

So he took a deep breath and told his father what had happened in the cell when he'd been alone but not alone, how God had come to him and shown him the door, and how he'd opened it and walked through to meet Jesus.

By the time he'd finished, the coastline of France had appeared. They sat there, father and son, huddled together as the sun appeared from behind the clouds and a rope of light shimmered on the water, pulling them towards the land.

If you've enjoyed this book, why not look out for...

By the same author:
He should have looked behind him
Tony Dobinson

Who killed Korman Ben Hator?

The Roman soldier is on his way
to report to his commanding
officer in Galilee when he is
murdered.

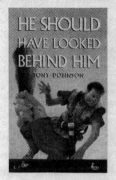

An innocent man is arrested and
charged.

His friend, Jeb, is determined to find out the truth even
though he puts himself into real danger from the
murderer.

Your challenge – should you decide to accept it – is to
work out who was the killer!

ISBN 1 85999 516 0

By the same author:
Hooked
Tony Dobinson

Running past the warning notices, running in panic, not looking where she was putting her feet... without stopping, she glanced around. But she couldn't see if he was following. Then her feet skidding on loose stones. For a moment she felt she was flying, then she was over, her body slamming into the edge of the cliff.

Down, down, nothing to hold on to. Then came the ledge. And, later, the voice. And the rope. And the star.

Can Angie's friendship rescue Alex? Get him off the hook?

ISBN 1 85999 413 X

Maria and the Street Kids
Lucy Moore

'I don't think my life can ever be quite the same again. You, Chico, always smiling even in the darkest times... You, Marco, with your sharp eyes and your longing for something I can't even begin to guess at... And Maria, with your courage and love and life... I won't forget you.'

When British businessman Peter is saved from the terrors of the night by Maria's gang of street kids, his eyes are opened to the harsh reality of their lives. On the streets of South America, every day is a struggle for survival, yet real love can still be found. But what can Peter really do for these forgotten children? And with danger and death only ever a heartbeat away, what does it really mean to 'Go with God'?

ISBN 1 85999 566 7

Friends First
Claire Pedrick and Andy Morgan

Does boy+girl really = sex?

This cunning handbook will help you sort through the muddle of boyfriends, girlfriends, best friends, ex-friends, church friends, school friends... we might even be able to help you out with your parents!

Dip in to get helpful advice from the Bible, youth leaders and people like yourself on how to deal with relationships in all their shapes and sizes.

ISBN 1 85999 644 2

(Available October 2002)

All of these titles are available from Christian bookshops, or online at www.scriptureunion.org.uk/publishing or call Mail Order direct on 01908 856006.